Dying In a Winter Wonderland

An Anthology of Winter Holiday Crime
Stories to Benefit the Toys for Tots™

Compiled and Edited
by
Tony Burton
Chief Editor, Crime and Suspense ezine

Foreword
by Stevenne Auerbach, Ph. D.
also known as "Dr. Toy"

These stories are works of fiction. Names, characters, places and incidents are either the product of the authors' imaginations or are used fictitiously, and any resemblance to actual persons, living or dead, business establishments, events or locales is entirely coincidental.

**Dying In a Winter Wonderland
An Anthology of Winter Holiday Crime Stories
to Benefit the Toys for Tots™**

ISBN-13: 978-1-60364-005-3

Copyright ©2008 Wolfmont Press
All Rights Reserved
Cover created by Tony Burton
Cover copyright ©2008 Tony Burton

This book may not be reproduced in whole or in part, by mimeograph, photocopy, or any other means, electronic or physical, without express written permission of the copyright holders. While the book in *toto* is copyright Wolfmont Press, the individual stories are copyrighted to their respective authors.

For information, contact:
info@wolfmont.com

or

Wolfmont Press
238 Park Drive NE
Ranger, GA 30734

Library of Congress Control Number: 2008936047

ISBN-13: 978-1-60364-005-3

Printed in the United States of America

Foreword

This year's Toys for Tots™ mystery anthology from Wolfmont Press, **DYING IN A WINTER WONDERLAND,** is hot off the press, in your hands, and ready to entertain you with unique stories of holiday mayhem.

Your purchase of this book helps fund the US Marines Toys for Tots™ Program that puts smiles on the faces of millions of deserving children as they receive their special gift of a toy. That is no mystery.

For the past two years talented authors have contributed to the previous Wolfmont anthologies, *By the Chimney With Care* and *Carols and Crimes, Gifts and Grifters*. Now those wonderful, altruistic folks at Wolfmont Press have another winning collection. Credit especially goes to the devoted Wolfmont Press editor Tony Burton, who has used his well-honed sleuthing ability to ferret out the best submissions.

As a result, underprivileged kids will be much happier. It's no mystery to this detective, that toys brighten faces, holiday spirits, and make a big difference in their young lives.

Tony Burton and I recall sometimes having very few toys as children except for boxes, clothespins, and a lot of imagination. We know what a great difference playthings make in the lives and hearts of children.

In the spirit of giving, we encourage booksellers to install toy collection barrels in their stores, contribute a share of the profits from the sales of this book, and spread more holiday cheer this year. There is no mystery: it's a fact, we can all do more to help children.

The crime yarns in this collection occur during the winter holiday season. You will find timely stories that are serious, humorous, mystical, and down-to-earth; all are well-written reflections on this year's theme.

So take a tip from me, your mystery guest, go out and buy multiple copies to give away to family and friends in their holiday stockings, office party grab bags, or fraternal fundraisers. Generously share the wealth of excellent mystery writing while giving to the most vulnerable, our future — our children.

How did Toys for Tots[TM] come to be? In 1947, Diane Hendricks made a special Raggedy Anne doll and asked her husband, Major Bill Hendricks, USMCR, to contribute it to an organization that gives toys to needy children. When he found out there was no such group, she asked him to start one. So he and a group of Marine Reservists collected and distributed the first toy collection. The tradition has continued ever since and your contribution helps to keep it alive and growing for generations to come.

For more information, go to
http://www.toysfortots.com

Stevanne Auerbach, PhD/Dr. Toy
Author, *Smart Play Smart Toys*
http://www.drtoy.com
San Francisco, CA

Table of Contents

A Mom for Christmas
    (Austin S. Camacho) 1
The Alternate Plan
    (Allan Ansorge) 19
A Merry Slay Ride
    (M. E. Kemp) 31
On the Sixth Night of Hanukah
    (Helen Schwartz) 49
Something Extra for Christmas
    (Radine Trees Nehring) 65
Gracie's Gift from the East
    (Gary R. Hoffman) 79
Happy Holidays Times Three
    (Peg Herring) 91
Taking Her Medicine
    (Tony Burton) 109
A Christmas Carole
    (Janice Alonso) 119
Just Call Me Nick
    (Terrie Farley Moran) 137
The Longest Night
    (S. M. Harding) 147
In the Nick of Time
    (Gayle Bartos-Pool) 165
Team Player
    (Marian Allen) 179

Contributor Profiles 189

A Mom for Christmas

Austin S. Camacho

Hannibal hated working during the holidays. In fact, he considered not answering the door after dark. But the knock was so insistent that his instincts told him it was someone in trouble. He sighed at Cindy, heaved up off the couch and opened the door.

His visitor couldn't have been more than eight or nine years old. She was as pretty as little Latina girls get, with her natural curls corralled into two rubber-banded ponytails. She looked him straight in the eye, wearing a stern expression.

"Are you Hannabubble Jones the private guy?"

Hannibal grinned, and heard a chuckle from behind him. "Yes, I guess I am. And you?"

"I'm Margarita. My mommy needs you to go help her get home for Christmas. She told me to give you this." Margarita presented a cookie jar shaped like a happy bear.

"Oh Hannibal, ask her to come in," Cindy called. Hannibal stepped aside and Margarita walked quietly into his apartment. She handed the cookie jar to Cindy and sat beside her.

"Christmas is only two days away," Hannibal said, taking the end of the couch. "How far away is your mommy?"

"Oh, she's just downtown," Margarita said. "She's a dancer, you know? She dances in the Queen's Castle. But when she called she said some bad men didn't want her to come home, and you were the knight that would come help her." Then she leaned in to give him a closer look. "You don't look like a knight to me."

"Oh, he's still in training," Cindy said, replacing the lid on the cookie jar. "Hannibal there's almost four hundred dollars in here."

"Last night's tips," Hannibal said. The little girl stared at him, and the fact that she looked so much like a shrunk down version of his girl friend made his decision easy. "Listen, Margarita, I know where your mom works. Were you home alone? Well, why don't you stay here with Miss Cindy and I'll go see if I can give your mom a ride home."

* * *

An hour later, Hannibal found a table toward the back at the Queen's Castle. The place had an upscale clientele due mostly to its location in Northwest DC, not far from Embassy Row. The Castle was an adult nightspot, dark and atmospheric, with "classy go-go girls," two stages and no cover. Hannibal was just one of many Black men in dark suits there that night. And presumably, Margarita's mother was one of the many girls dancing that night. But which one?

The club, and the girls, were decorated for the holidays. Colored lights, tinsel and poinsettias on the tables took care of the club. The girls playing waitress were decked out in Santa outfits, complete with red satin bikinis and heels, fur-edged hats and big white beards. Those taking their turns on stage wore tiny green elf costumes. Amber Martinez could be any one of them.

That is, until the music stopped. One dancer headed toward a dark corner, presumably to shake like a bowlful of jelly for a private audience. A big Latino in biker boots and jeans was helping the other girl off the stage. As they headed toward the door a second man joined them. He was taller and thinner, with a scar along the right side of his nose. His face betrayed a native viciousness Hannibal recognized. Even if this wasn't the woman he was looking for he'd want to smack that guy. He stood and set an intercept course.

"Hannibal Jones." A woman with obsidian skin and eyes took his arm, smiling brightly as she walked with him. "You're not a regular in my place. You're not going to start any trouble are you?"

"You must be Foxxy, the owner," Hannibal said, not slowing down. "I'm afraid some trouble has already started without me. I'll try to keep it low key, but you should be prepared to do damage control."

"Ahhh… two escorts for one of my dancers," Foxxy said. "And she seems to be resisting. I see, and these boys look serious. Okay, do your thing, honey, and if it all works out, come to the door behind the bar on the east wall."

Foxxy peeled away and Hannibal sped up enough to reach the door just in front of his target trio. He staggered slightly, let his gloved hand slip on the doorknob, and walked into the door. The heavier man laid a hand on Hannibal's left shoulder and pulled to toss him to the side. Hannibal spun with him, slamming his right fist into the man's stomach. The thug crumpled to his knees. The taller man was faster, shoving the girl behind him and pulling a switchblade.

Hannibal stepped back and to the side. His right foot snapped out into the tall man's ribs. A sharp right hook put the man into the wall and onto the floor.

Only a handful of patrons turned away from the entertainment long enough to see any of the action. By then Hannibal was dragging the girl by her wrist to the bar and thru a half-width door behind it. A narrow passage led them to a storeroom stacked with cases of liquor. The girl moved to a low table and dropped onto a chair.

"You are Jones?"

"I am. And if you're Amber Martinez you're too young to have sent that messenger."

Amber smiled. "Then Margarita found you. She is such a good girl. And yes, I was very young when she was born. Can you get me home to her?"

"We'll see," Hannibal said. "Is scarface out there likely to have friends around?" Taking in the girl's dark eyes and long, straight black hair, Hannibal thought she reminded him of an Eagles song. Not because she was living life in the fast lane, but because she was, as the song goes, terminally pretty.

"Garcia is a coyote," Amber said. "He has many men who will do as he says. He helped my family come here but I must get away from him."

"Are you telling me you're illegal?" Foxxy asked, stepping into the back room.

"The coyote brought my parents and me in, but Margarita was born here. She is an American. And I am all she has. That is why I have paid their blackmail, but when they told me they would take me away tonight I knew I had to break away and hoped you would help me."

"You said your parents came with you," Hannibal said. "I'm thinking there's more to this story."

Amber nodded and looked down. "My father worked hard like so many who come here. As long as you get a social security card and pay your taxes no one notices that you are illegal. He invested well and saved a lot of money and put it in different bank accounts. And once a year he sent me to visit family in Colombia. But this year while I was back home Daddy died. Knowing my father would not be paying them, the people who usually help me turned their backs on me."

"Then how'd you get back to the states, honey?" Foxxy asked.

"Garcia knew how to get me in, but only if I helped him bring drugs into the country. I had no choice. Margarita was here. But now they demand money or they will turn me in for drug smuggling. And my sponsor would stop helping me get my citizenship if he thought I was a criminal."

Hannibal doubted anybody smuggling humans into the country would talk to the police about anything, but they could discuss that later.

"So all you want to do is get the money your father left you, get to someplace safe and raise your daughter," he said.

"Yes," Amber said. "Mr. Perez has paid the blackmail for me and tried to keep me hidden. My father's will stipulates that his entire estate comes to me when I turn twenty-five."

Hannibal had to fight to keep his jaw from dropping. "You're not even 25? When's your birthday?"

"I was born on Christmas Day," Amber said, flashing a sheepish grin.

"Which is why they wanted to snatch you today," he said, almost to himself. He looked toward the door.

"Don't even think about fighting your way out," Foxxy said. "Can't have you shooting up my place. Bad for business."

"But you know this Garcia will have an army here by now," Hannibal said. "How about we call the police and get escorted out peaceful-like?"

"Oh hell no." Foxxy snapped, moving her neck around in that odd way women do when they get emotional. "You gone bring the man in here and ruin my Christmas spirit? No, baby, come on with mama and let me show you how this works." Foxxy led Hannibal to a back corner of the storeroom and pushed a stack of boxes aside to reveal a back door. It opened into a long, dark tunnel.

"This comes out in the next block."

"You'll understand if I don't take your word for it, right?" Hannibal knew Foxxy's reputation: a player, driven by self-interest. For the right price she'd certainly lead him into a trap.

"Go head and check it out," she said, not at all offended. "You can pop out there and walk to the Metro, and come back for your car tomorrow when things is cool."

"It's worth a try," Hannibal said, "even though Garcia might have his boys on the lookout there too."

"I got an idea for that," Foxxy said, flicking her inch-long dagger nails toward the tunnel. "Now go ahead and get your bearings. I'll have her all set when you get back."

Hannibal raced down the dark, narrow passage considering all the possible things that could go wrong. If he got back and the door was locked he could easily kick it in. If he encountered trouble at the far end of the tunnel, well, that was what his Sig Sauer P-220 was for. But when he stepped out into the moonlight there was nobody around. a half-inch of snow covered the ground, so a quick scan assured him that no one had been near the exit all evening.

Reassured, he hurried back to the storeroom. As he opened the door, Foxxy thrust a hideous plaid sport coat at him.

"Here, give me your jacket and put this on."

"What, you think nobody will know me if I'm not in a black suit? What about Amber?"

"Well, they're looking for an elf," Foxxy said. But now the woman at her side wore the waitress' Santa suit, complete with heavy fake beard and hat.

"Good thinking," Hannibal said, pulling the sport coat on. "If we take it slow we should be able to walk right past any of Garcia's guys."

He grabbed the girl's hand and darted down the passage. When they stepped into the crisp open air he still saw no observers so they turned south and walked hand-in-hand toward the Metro station. His mind was divided between keeping his walk casual and scanning the area for anyone paying too much attention to them. A block from the station they started across the street and she tripped on the curb.

"Son of a..." she snapped out, and that was enough. Hannibal hauled her to her feet and yanked off the beard. That voice had not been Amber's, and the cute Hispanic face now revealed was more mature than the one he admired in the Queen's Castle.

"Is this Foxxy's idea of a joke?" Hannibal asked.

"Hey, Amber didn't want to go with you," the girl said, "So Foxxy asked me to take her place. Besides, wouldn't you rather have a grown woman for Christmas instead of that child?"

Hannibal pushed her aside, thinking they'd both been hustled, and jogged back toward the Queen's Castle. It was so obvious in hindsight. The kidnappers must have paid Foxxy to let them haul the girl away to begin with. When Hannibal showed up she faced a dilemma. She didn't want to lose her payoff, but she knew a battle could wreck her club. This way she gets her money, and with the girl gone she knew Hannibal wouldn't demolish her place.

And he knew Amber would be long gone by now, but he might be able to get some useful leads from Foxxy. She'd want to cash in twice, and anyway, she owed him now.

As the club came into view Hannibal crouched behind a parked car. A tall man was walking away from the entrance to the tunnel Hannibal had used. It was hard to tell from there but he could be Garcia. Maybe he returned to finish his business with Foxxy. If so, Hannibal could follow him to Amber.

The tall man started walking away. Hannibal moved toward him, closing the gap without betraying any rush. Could his luck be this good?

He came even with the secret door when he was within half a block of his quarry. Stepping past the entrance his peripheral vision picked up an unmoving figure in the shadows. Female, very dark, one long-nailed hand outstretched. Apparently Garcia *had* returned to finish his business with Foxxy. Hannibal couldn't help her now. And if Garcia was the reason she was face down in an alley that increased his concern for Amber. He rushed forward.

The tall man was stepping into a little red car, maybe a Ford Focus. In a few steps Hannibal would be able to get the plate number. Then he could track the killer down. But then the tall man looked up. Hannibal recognized Garcia, and he recognized Hannibal too because he raised his hand to point at him and there was a pistol already in it.

Hannibal fell backward, the snow helping his

feet slip out from under him. He didn't hear the gun go off, but he heard the bullet zip past overhead. The sound from a silenced .22 didn't carry far on the winter wind.

By the time Hannibal had his automatic out Garcia was in the car and moving away. He watched until the exhaust trail dissipated, then ran back to the Queen's Castle back door.

Hannibal's knees chilled as he knelt in the snow, more aware of seeing his breath because none came from Foxxy. Gloved fingertips confirmed the lack of pulse. The snow drew the spreading red pool out away from her in all directions. The entry wound would be underneath, in her belly. A gut shot was unnecessary cruelty.

Then Hannibal's eyes followed her arm, outstretched, reaching for help or maybe for her killer. No. Her long nails weren't just scratching in the snow. She had died trying to help him get her killer.

"What happened, Foxxy?" he whispered. "Did you try to follow them? To get a lead I'd pay for? Or some info that might protect you? Whatever, Garcia wasn't going to leave you as a witness. You crossed me but maybe you tried to make it up."

* * *

"He left her there in the snow?" Mother Washington asked. Hannibal's neighbor, Monte's grandmother, was watching the little girl.

"Like he had a choice?" Monte asked with a shrug. Nothing shocks teenagers. "What, he was going to sit there and spend the night with five-oh? Besides,

A Mom for Christmas

cops get in this, the Mex thug gets nervous and shanks the girl."

"Can you find this man?" Mother Washington asked.

Before Hannibal could answer, Margarita wandered into the living room, rubbing her eyes.

"Morning, sleepy head," Cindy said. "I've never seen a girl your age stay in bed past 10 before."

Margarita looked over at Mother Washington's big, decorated tree and remembered where she was and why. "Did you find my mommy?"

"Not yet I'm afraid," Cindy said, welcoming the girl into her arms. "But a nice lady saw the car she was in and, well, she wrote down the license number where Hannibal could see it. Our friend at the Department of Motor Vehicles told us who owns the car and we're going to visit him. He'll know where your mommy is."

Margarita hugged Cindy's neck, but turned her big brown eyes like searchlights on Hannibal. "Will you bring me my mommy for Christmas?"

When Hannibal hesitated, Mother Washington spoke for him.

"Don't you worry, child. This man, he don't let nobody down."

* * *

Hannibal was surprised to find Carlos Perez in his law office on the afternoon of Christmas Eve. A one-man law firm on Pennsylvania Avenue had to be successful. Maybe he just had no place to go. Cindy didn't either, and when she learned Hannibal was meeting a lawyer she insisted on joining him.

The round, tan face that answered the door wore a full head of black, slicked-down hair. He was a couple of inches shorter than Hannibal's six feet but he still bore a lawyer's natural arrogance.

"Can I help you?" He retained just enough of an accent to betray his heritage.

"I'm Hannibal Jones, and investigator, and this is Cyntia Santiago of Baylor, Truman and Ray."

"An attorney and a," Perez gave Hannibal a hard look, "I assume you're a private investigator or you would have identified yourself as a cop. What can you possibly want today?"

"We're here about Amber Martinez," Cindy said.

Perez blanched. "Amber? Is she all right?"

"If we could talk inside?" At Hannibal's request Perez stepped back, moving to his desk as if for security.

"How do you know Ms Martinez?" Cindy asked while Hannibal closed the door behind them.

"I've known Amber for years," Perez said, popping a scotch decanter. When his two guests declined he poured himself three fingers of the liquid. "Her parents immigrated when she was pregnant so her child could be born in the U.S. Her mother passed not long after they arrived. Her father was a rather gifted accountant, and he came to this country with quite a bit of money. I've handled his personal finances since they arrived."

"Where is she now?" Hannibal asked, standing beside the desk as Perez dropped into his chair.

A Mom for Christmas

"Why do you think I know?" Perez asked. "In fact, how did you know to come to me about this?"

"Funny you should ask," Hannibal said, thinking it was funny that he didn't ask a lot sooner. "She was seen getting into one of your cars last night. A red Ford Focus."

"Oh. Well. That's the car I let her drive from time to time. she hasn't much money."

"Actually, I understand her father left her quite a bit of money," Hannibal said, "but she can't get at it until her birthday. And I'm doubting anybody knows where the cash is except you."

"What are you saying?" Perez asked. "Do you think I've got her stashed in my home?"

Hannibal knew better than that. He had already searched Perez's home.

"No, but I'm wondering if you know where she is. And if you have a relationship with a Mexican thug named Garcia. And just what Mr. Martinez died of."

He was shooting at shapes in the dark, but Perez flinched at Garcia's name. And with the mention of Martinez' death Hannibal knew he had hit something. Sweat broke out on Perez' forehead.

But he was a lawyer. He recovered quickly.

"How dare you accuse me of such monstrous things? You have no evidence that I've done anything wrong. I'll sue you."

He was right of course. Hannibal had no way of knowing if Amber's father was murdered. He knew Perez was the key to finding her, but he didn't have

13

enough to squeeze him. Then Cindy spoke up.

"We'll just exhume the body."

Perez snapped to his feet. "Preposterous. You have no reasonable cause."

"Sit down, counselor," Cindy said in her courtroom voice. "You know that a lawyer in the right firm can get a judge to order an exhumation based on circumstantial evidence and a strong suspicion. And that order will freeze the assets of the deceased until we can get to the bottom of all this."

Perez dropped back into his chair and drained his glass. He was crumbling quickly, unable to see a way out.

"You can't do that. He'll kill her."

"He, being Garcia?" Hannibal asked. "I bet he's the friendly soul who got her back into the states. He blackmailed her, and you pretended to pay it to secure her trust, thinking she'd repay you with her inheritance. But when it became clear she'd rather run than give up the money Garcia decided to grab her and force her to draw the money out and give it to him."

"Yes," Perez said, his face dripping now. "Yes, and I'm a victim too. He forced me to..."

"Don't even try," Hannibal said. "None of this could have happened without the one man who knows where all the accounts are. You."

"No matter what you believe, they will kill her if you or the police get involved. And if they can't get the money they'll kill me too."

"Who gives a rat's butt?" Hannibal asked,

grabbing Perez' collar with both hands. "I figure you had a hand in one murder and maybe two. I think you're in this up to your ears and could fry with the shooter when the police catch him. But I'm on the clock and all I really care about is getting one mother home in time for her daughter to open her presents. So, the way I see it I got two good options. I can beat Amber's location out of you, which would be fun but time consuming. Or, you can lead me to her and hope a court mistakes your cowardice for cooperation."

* * *

Twilight was creeping in by the time Perez was driving his Beemer down the dirt trail toward his summer home on Maryland's Eastern shore. During the two hour drive to Cambridge Hannibal held the gun relaxed but ready in his lap, especially when Perez made the phone call to let his partners know he was coming out to try to persuade Amber to sign over the accounts to him voluntarily.

When Perez parked beside the familiar red Focus Hannibal scanned the house. One level, maybe three bedrooms, lots of trees close in, the long driveway being the only approach to the house.

"How many?"

"Two of them," Perez said. "Listen, these men are animals. They'll shoot you as soon as they see you. Why don't I go to the front door and distract them. You can go to the back door and get the drop on them. Maybe you can get to her out without any violence."

Hannibal nodded. "Okay, we can try it your way.

But if something pops off, hit the floor and stay out of the line of fire."

Both men left the car. Perez walked toward the front door. Hannibal disappeared into the shadows.

Perez stopped in front of the door for a minute as if he were rethinking his options. He looked around one last time, squared his shoulders, took a deep breath, and knocked on the door - three loud thumps. Then he returned to his car.

As Perez reached for the car door handle, Hannibal grabbed the back of his collar and yanked him toward the back of the house.

"Change of plans. Let's both be heroes."

Perez stumbled forward, unable to get his balance. Hannibal dragged him on, in front of himself. They were approaching the back door when fire burst from a back windows. Both men were slapped back onto the grass. Reaching around, Hannibal found the entry wound in the center of Perez's chest.

Only an amateur would have set up such an obvious trap, and the fact that Perez paid for his sneaky stupidity didn't bother Hannibal one bit.

Squirming out from under the body, Hannibal started toward the house when Perez's cell phone rang. Hannibal found it in his coat pocket and flipped it open.

"Jorge got him. Come on in."

Hannibal grunted a response, closed the phone and went to the front door. When it opened he shoved his pistol into the scarred face he recognized. He could see another man on the sofa.

"It was a clumsy play, Garcia," Hannibal said. "You're going to need a new lawyer, and the place is surrounded by the police who followed us out here. Now bring me the girl."

Garcia's eyes narrowed, searching his memory. "I know you. I seen you before. Yeah, in the Castle. You ain't no cop."

Garcia reached to his waistband. When his pistol came into view Hannibal put a forty-caliber hole in his right arm.

"Thanks, stupid." Then to the man on the couch, "You stupid too?" The second man raised his hands as Hannibal kicked Garcia's gun out the door and stepped over him. As he passed the second man he swung his gun back and down into his temple. He slumped onto the floor and stayed there.

Amber's eyes widened when Hannibal entered the room. She was tied to the bed but he freed her in seconds.

"How did you find me?" she asked.

"Long story, messy in parts," he said. "I'll tell you on the way home. Christmas is only hours away and I got to get you back to my little client. It should be a nice ride though, in your Christmas present from Perez, a nice BMW."

Copyright © 2008 Austin S. Camacho

The Alternate Plan

Allan Ansorge

"Maybe we ought to try something else, Moss; it's really cold in this alley."

Snow flew from the brim of Moss's hat as he wheeled on his partner, Gibby. "What do you mean, cold? You just got back here from the restaurant."

"I know, but my right hand is freezing"

"Well, put it in your pocket."

"It's in my pocket, that's why it's cold. I'm holding the gun with it."

"Let go of the gun, Gibby; you don't have to hold it. Go back across the street to the restaurant and warm your hand. I'll stay on watch, It shouldn't be much longer. That Santa's pot should be nearly full."

"I can't, the guy running the place told me to get out and stay out."

"Why would he say that? What did you do?"

"Nothing! I was just standing there inside the door and he said if I wasn't gonna buy something I should get the hell out."

"So why didn't you buy something?"

Gibby's eyes rolled. "I couldn't buy something, Moss. I haven't got any money. That's why were gonna rob the Santa, right?"

"Tell you what, Gib, take a walk through the toy store next to the restaurant. Browse a little and get yourself warm; when you come back, I'll take a turn."

The little man squeezed past Moss's bulk and was just about clear of the alley entrance when Moss pulled him back.

"Look out, Gibby. That's a squad car coming down the street. Duck back in here. We don't want any cops seeing us in the neighborhood, if you get my drift."

"Gotcha, Moss." Gibby peeked under Moss's arm as the squad car drew up to the curb opposite the alley. A uniformed officer exited the car and shuffled through the street slush to the trunk area. A twist of his keys and he removed a large basket wrapped in clear plastic from the car's trunk. He sat it on the fender of the car while he checked street addresses.

"That's Mike McCaffery, Moss. How the heck did he know we was here?"

"Shush, Gibby. He doesn't know we're here. He can't have found out the warden let us out early already. It looks like he is taking that basket to that door next to the toy store. Yup he's knocking now. Hey, look at that, he's giving that basket to some lady and that little kid. It must be some kinda Christmas basket."

"I wonder how we could get a basket like that, Moss. I bet it has all kinds of stuff to eat, good stuff, Christmas stuff."

"The kid is tearing it open now. Naw, I can't believe it. The kid pulled out a stinking sweater. What the heck kind of Christmas treat is that for a little kid? You know, Gib, I thought McCaffery was smarter than

The Alternate Plan

that. Now I'm really embarrassed that clown ever put us in the slammer."

"It looks like a nice heavy sweater, Moss."

"But a sweater for Christmas, Gib! You know what I mean. That ain't nothing for a little guy like that to get. He should be getting toys and candy! Duck back, Gib, McCaffery is turning this way."

Mike McCaffery climbed back into his squad and slowly rolled away from the curb, leaving a wake of "thank you's" and waves behind him.

"Okay, Gib, the lady is going back in. Take a trip to the toy store for a warm up. Try not to get noticed this time." Moss whispered to Gibby's departing back, "Don't hold the cold gun."

The small boy pulled the sweater over his head and made the six step journey to the window of the toy store. Gibby saw the reflection of the store window's lights and glitter in the boy's eyes as he held the door so they could both enter. The boy took a half step back and gave a small shake of his head. Gibby made the correct assumption: The boy was as welcome in the toy store as he was in the restaurant.

The narrow boards of the white oak floor creaked under Gibby's shoes as the would-be robber stepped over the threshold. He glanced back through the front window, and his eyes met those of the boy peeking through the decorations and toys on display.

A short, stocky man greeted Gibby with a, "What do you need, mister?" His tone was gruff and didn't strike Gibby as being filled with the Christmas

Eve spirit he expected.

"Just browsing for the minute, thank you."

"Well you better make up your mind quick. I'm planning on closing in about twenty minutes."

The man stepped around Gibby, waving his arms and shouting to be heard through the store window. "Get away from here, go back home. You're scaring away customers, you little twerp." Brushing past Gibby, he mumbled, "Damn kid next door, he makes the place look like something out of Dickens. You know, he asked me if I could set aside that bike and he could pay me a quarter a week on it. I pay him a quarter to sweep out the store and he wants me to finance the bike yet too, with my own quarter. Kids, they want everything nowadays."

Gibby saw the small face reappear in the corner of the window as soon as the man's back was turned. "That bike's pretty small for him, ain't it?"

"You don't know much about bikes, do you, mister?"

"No, I never had one."

"That's a girl's bike. It's pink for a little girl. See the training wheels? I guess he wants to buy it for his sister."

"What does a bike like that cost?" Gibby's hand slipped into his pocket and felt cold steel.

"Should go for 80 bucks, but since it's Christmas Eve, I'll let you have it for 75 plus the tax a'coarse."

Gibby's hand tightened on the pistols grip. He glanced back at the window to the small face and a

The Alternate Plan

chill went up his spine. Thoughts whirled in Gibby's head, no there has to be a better way. "I don't have a little girl, just curious. Guess I best be head'n home. You have a nice holiday."

Gibby didn't wait for the man's mumbled reply. He ignored the stare of the small boy as he crossed the street to the alley and the waiting Moss. "Moss, you ever had a bike?"

"No, Gibby, I never did, but I got something to tell you."

"Me too Moss. I just met the meanest bastard on earth."

"Later, Gib. Watch Santa over there for a few minutes."

"But Moss—"

"Quiet, Gib, just watch. See the couple coming around the corner? Watch what happens when they get to Santa's kettle."

"They dropped a couple of bills in the slot. That's nice of them, and good for us, ain't it Moss?"

"Keep watching, Gibby. Catch what happens when they walk away. See! See! That damn Santa has the hole in the pot rigged so he can pull the money back out. There he goes. He's sticking the money into his pocket. That creep is skimming from the pot, do you believe it? Those people think the're donating to a good cause and he is robbing from them and the charity."

"You know Moss, you'd think you could trust a Santa Claus."

23

"Gibby, you know that's not the real Santa right?"

"Yeah, Moss, I know, but it's the thought of it that's disturb'n. I mean, we were going to rob him, 'cause that's what we do, but he's stealing from both sides. That makes him twice as bad as we are. Doesn't it, Moss?"

"Well, not quite, Gib. This is the way I see it. If we go over there and take the money away from that bum that he already stole, then it's not like we are stealing it from the people who thought they were donating it, 'cause it's really already stolen."

Gibby's eyes wandered in no particular direction, he was certain that there was something wrong about Moss's plan, but he was having a problem pinning it down. Moss gave him a nudge in the back and whispered, "Now put your hand on the gun Gibby. Lets go over there and give that crook a lesson on the spirit of Christmas."

Gibby scurried across the street, taking on the attitude of an avenging angel. Moss trailed behind, hopping on one foot. The snow and slush had found its way through the hole in the sole of his right shoe.

Small bubbles of saliva formed in the corners of Gibby's mouth as he attempted to articulate a coherent sentence expressing his anger at the Santa's activities. His hand shaking on the gun, he was waving the whole right side of his jacket in Santa's direction. The Santa was certain he was being accosted by some sort of lunatic until Moss hopped over the curb and

The Alternate Plan

interceded.

"We have been watching you, Mr. Claus, and we know you're a thieving crumb. This is what is going to happen. You reach into your pocket where you stuck all the dough you skimmed from the pot here, and hand it over. Then you take your kettle back where it came from and turn in your suit and beard. By the way, if my friend here ever sees you on the street doing this again, he could get very upset."

The Santa glanced at Gibby, who was bouncing about, desperately attempting to remove the gun from his pocket to emphasize Moss's tirade.

The Santa eyes widened with fear as he blurted out, "How do I know this nut has a gun?"

There was the sound of tearing material and the gun appeared in Gibby's hand. The catch for the clip caught on a hole in his pocket and the clip and bullets fell into the snow as he waved the automatic in the direction of Santa's nose. Santa was smart enough to know there could still be one bullet in the chamber and was handing over the stolen cash as Moss continued his lecture.

"You'd be smart not to report this to anyone. Stealing from you is one thing stealing from poor kids and orphans is another. I'm sure you would rather not have that come out, would you? You could end up doing twice the time we would get."

Santa gathered up his stand and kettle and ran off in what he hoped was the direction of Santa headquarters to resign. Gibby, on an adrenaline high, trotted after Moss back to the alley.

As Moss flattened the bills for counting, he asked, "Gibby, what was it you were saying about some bastard before?"

"Oh yeah, the guy from the toy store, he was being really nasty to the boy, especially considering it is Christmas and all. Did you ever have a bike, Moss?"

"What boy, Gib? Do you think you need a bike? I'm not following here. Fifty-one, fifty-two..."

"The boy with the sweater: He wants a bike. Not for him, he wants it for his sister."

"Fifty-five, fifty-six. That's nice, Gib, that the little guy wants to get a bike for her. Thirty-seven. Damn, now I have to start over."

"I was thinking, Moss."

Moss cut a hard look in Gibby's general direction. "Thinking, Gibby? Thinking what?"

"I been thinking about what you said about Santa. You know, stealing from both ends and how rotten he was. I think you got it wrong, Moss. I think we might be doing the same thing, and that makes us just as bad as him."

Moss blinked his eyes to adjust to the new darkness of the alley as the lights from the restaurant faded. He found himself talking to the spot where he assumed Gibby was still standing. "Are you suggesting we give this money up to the first guy that walks down the street?"

"No, that won't work; it isn't his money any more than it's ours."

The Alternate Plan

"We can't take it to the Santa. That crook is long gone by now."

"No, I guess we can't."

"The way I see it, Gib, we deserve this money. We kind of rescued it. You know, Gibby, people gave this money for a worthy cause. We're a worthy cause. We have no food, no money, and on top of that we have nowhere to sleep. We're worthy, Gib, as worthy as anybody I have ever seen. It's not our fault they let us out early. Is it, Gib? Tell me, is that our fault?"

"Guess not, Moss. It's just you were the one who said the sweater kid ought to get something better for Christmas. You know, Moss, we been broke before. We can do broke. We could go to the mission and get some soup and they'll let us sleep there until we come up with something else."

Moss dropped the wad of bills to the ground when a voice from the back of alley whispered, "Merry Christmas, boys."

Moss dove for the bills and shouted, "RUN GIBBY, RUN!"

"Don't bother. I know who you are and I can find you anytime I want to," the voice said, louder this time.

Moss dusted snow from his coat as he righted himself. "That you, McCaffery? How did you get here so fast?"

Mike's flashlight shone on Gibby and Moss as he advanced toward them. "That Santa's act caught my eye when I was making a delivery across the street. By the way, Gibby, you're right, the toy store guy is a bastard. You'd be surprised how the echo from this alley carries across the street."

"We'll have to keep that in mind in the future." Moss looked at his wrist as if his long ago pawned watch were still there. "Oh my, look at the time, gotta run, Mike, nice chatting. Gotta go."

"Stay where you are, you two. You both know this isn't the way that this has to end. I can't let you get away with an armed robbery. Well, almost armed. I picked up your cartridges and clip Gibby. You know you should be more careful with a gun, even if the shells are lying on the sidewalk. What do you think we should do about this situation, guys?"

Gibby took the lead. "Whatever you say, Mike, is okay with me."

"I can't believe I'm saying this, but for once I agree with you, Gibby. If you don't have the money, there is no evidence. No evidence, no robbery. Let's go buy a bike."

Gibby was practically skipping across the street in front of Moss, who trudged alongside of Mike. While negotiations for the bike improved when lead by Mike in his uniform, the would-be thieves were still eight dollars short. In a moment of weakness, Mike agreed to bear the burden of the difference under the assurance of his conspirators he would not be in sight at the delivery.

Moss and Gibby had a little spring in their step as they made their way back to the alley. "We did something good tonight, Moss. You should be happy about that. I'm sure Mike will give us a ride back to the jail: I don't think he'll make us walk in all this snow."

"You're a real Christmas pip, Gibby, don't ever forget it."

The back door of Mike's cruiser opened as they neared it. "Hurry up guys we're late."

Gibby was yet again puzzled. "Does the jail close early for Christmas, Mike?"

The car's tires spun and they were out of the alley. "We're not going there. We're headed to my place to find you a jacket that isn't ripped to shreds, then dinner."

Moss and Gibby exchanged confused glances. In near unison they asked, "You're making dinner for us?"

"Not quite, I have a friend, Sharon—you'll like her—she keeps her diner open on Christmas Eve so that people without families can go there for a free dinner. I guess that includes us, fellas. By the way, Moss, don't you ever refer to me as a clown again."

"The echo in the alley?"

"Right."

Copyright © 2008 Allan Ansorge

A Merry Slay Ride

M.E. Kemp

Squint-eyed Harmen's sleigh was one of many that drew up to the stout brick home of Gerritt van Wiesal and his wife, Anneke Van Kleeck that was, the Dutch wives of Albany keeping their own names. It was the charming custom to pay New Year's visits to friends and neighbors. Gerritt and Anneke were a popular couple, the former being of a genial and garrulous disposition; the latter respected as the daughter of one of the founders of the colony. Squint-eyed Harmen's sleigh was one of many that drove up to the stout brick home, but Squint-eyed Harmen's sleigh was the only sleigh with a dead body in it.

The brown mare pranced up the icy drive and around the snow-packed curve to the front steps to discharge its passenger. The brown mare waited patiently but the passenger didn't move. The groom that caught the reins gave a loud cry and stood frozen like Lot. Squint-eyed Harmen lay on his side, a trickle of blood dribbling from his mouth and a huge blotch of rust spreading across his brown woolen cloak. Pale blue eyes stared unseeing beyond the groom's shoulder. The groom cried out once more and servants came running. The farm's steward pried the reins from the groom's frozen fingers and led the sleigh around back to the stables. He sent one of the servants into the house.

From the corner of my eye I caught a glimpse of

a servant speaking into the ear of our host, but I thought nothing of that and turned my attention back to the elderly gentleman who told me a cure for chilblains, that I should rub the limbs with fresh urine. I felt a heavy hand upon my shoulder and Gerritt whispered into my ear.

"Mrs Henry, may I have a word with you, please?" Gerritt huffed his consonants, a sign that he was upset.

"Of course." I made my excuses to the elderly gentleman, thanked him for his advice, curtsied and turned to Gerritt.

The Dutchman wanted more than a word, I gathered, as he pulled me away. "You are needed." He spoke in a brusque tone, quite unlike his usual good nature, and I followed him meekly. He led me through a busy kitchen full of wonderful scents like ginger and spices and spits of sizzling meats. We went out the back door to the stables, where I saw a sleigh with several servants hovering over it.

As we neared the sled I could see a person lying in it. A tipsy driver? But no, Gerritt would not have called me out for a drunken driver, which was not an uncommon sight. Up close I could see the reason for the commotion. Could the man have frozen in his sled? I was about to witness my first — not my first dead body, but my first in a sleigh. I peered over the side. I knew Squint-eyed Harmen by sight and by reputation.

"Hetty, what do you think?" Gerritt puffed.

A Merry Slay Ride

I walked around the sleigh, my eyes searching for any oddities. I found only one. "Look at his position, Gerritt," I said, stopping by the sled's bench. "He wasn't driving. There's no sign of a struggle, so he must have been with someone he knew. Who did he accompany on his rounds?" I didn't bother to ask who might have killed him. As I say, I knew the man by reputation. Squint-eyed Harmen was a shiftless, lazy, good-for-nothing; a liar and a thief. He'd stood before the magistrates on more than one occasion. Still, even Squint-eyed Harmen deserved to start the New Year with a chance for redemption.

Gerritt shook his head in the negative, the servants following his lead.

"Come, let's have a look at the body. Where can we put the poor wretch?" I had no wish to ruin the New Year's calls for Anneke by carrying a corpse through a house full of guests.

Gerritt shook his shaggy head. "The dairy has a table...."

"Your dear wife won't thank you for that," I said, thinking of the cream and butter tubs inside. I gestured to a small outbuilding. "How about the tool shed? It has a table, does it not?"

Gerritt nodded. "And we can build the coffin with Harmen right there to measure. Very convenient, I think it." The servants bobbed their heads in agreement. The Dutch were practical to a fault.

The steward took charge of moving the body, while Gerritt and I waited, stamping our feet on the packed-snow ground. "You're good at solving puzzles, Hetty. Who do you think killed him?"

"I'll perhaps know more when I've examined the body," I said. "We'll need to trace his steps. That shouldn't be hard." Sleighs had to stay in the ridges cut by previous runners. The steward beckoned and we followed into the work shed. Harmen's corpse was laid upon the rough surface of a wooden table.

"Pull back his cloak," I directed one of the men. "Let's take a look at the wound."

"Stabbed to the heart," Gerritt said, stating the obvious.

The knife penetrated through a buff-colored waistcoat and a white shirt with a plain band that was relatively clean. Except for the great splotch of scarlet.

"All dressed up for making calls," I said.

Gerritt pointed a stubby finger to the waistcoat. "Something's pinned there."

There was indeed a ribbon pinned to the coat; a pink, blood-spattered ribbon. "Had he a sweetheart?" I wrinkled my nose in distaste. What woman would have anything to do with the shiftless little worm? Harmen could hardly be called handsome, even without the squint.

Gerritt spat in disgust. "Not any of our women would have to do with him. The English ladies are even more finicky, I think." He unpinned the ribbon and handed it to me.

I held it gingerly between my two fingers. Poor Harmen — even in death women avoided him. I noted the ribbon was bent and frayed along each edge. It was about the length to tie up a bundle a love letters, I thought. How would Squint-eyed Harmen come by a bundle of love letters? "I think we have to go through his things," I said. I had no wish to touch anything of Squint-eyed Harmen, but duty is a stern mistress.

Gerritt left to tell Anneke that there was a dead body in the woodshed. I asked the steward to make Gerritt's sleigh ready. Soon I was huddled under a warm bearskin robe, Gerritt handling the reins as we flew over snow-covered fields.

Harmen rented a room in a respectable house near the English fort. Mistress Skoggins, the owner, agreed to let us see the room only after a few coins passed between us. "What's he been up to?" she asked, leading us to the back of the house where the roof sloped down to nearly meet the ground. "You can be sure I made him pay me for six months in advance."

"Six months?" I could not keep the surprise from my voice. Where had Harmon earned the money for his rent?

"Well, he had the cash. I couldn't refuse him, now could I?" The lady spoke with asperity. "Said as he'd a notion to keep warm this winter. He's been here since November. No meals, though. I told him I don't do meals.' She lifted the latch to the tiny room. The door had no lock that I could see. "The truth is, I didn't see much of the man." She thrust open the door. "Where's he gone to? If he's run off, he's lost his money, that's all I say." She crossed her arms as if to defy us.

"The gentleman won't be coming back. You may rent out his room with no fear," I said. Gerritt and I entered the little room, both our backs bent, the roof was so low. Mistress Skoggins stood just outside the door, arms crossed, like a Greek sentinel. I began to shiver; there was no fireplace in the room so how could Harmen have stayed warm here? The room's contents consisted of a cot with moth-eaten blankets and an old chest. I didn't particularly want to touch either but I choose the cot. I pulled off and folded a faded red blanket with a faded blue stripe, which I recognized as a blanket for the native trade. I laid it neatly on the floor. Next I took off and folded a linen sheet full of rips and holes. Mistress Skoggins did not stint on her guests' linens, I thought with irony. The mattress was of cornhusks covered by canvas. I pounded upon it to scare the lice and to spot any extra lumps.

"Careful there, if you put a hole in the mattress you'll have to pay for it," Mistress called out.

I ignored her and kept on pounding and prodding. Gerritt slammed the lid of the chest and came over to see me. "Come, Hetty, if you have not found anything we should go."

I shrugged and followed him out the door. I thought it a wonder that Mistress Skoggins had any boarders at all since she treated them so shabbily, but I realized that her location near the fort no doubt brought soldiers and their families to stay close by.

I pulled my cape about me as I stepped out the door. The outside air might be cold but it was crisp

A Merry Slay Ride

and not as bone chilling as that house. My frustration must have shown in my face. Gerritt took my arm and helped me back into the sleigh. I pulled the bearskin robe up to my nose. When I turned to look at Gerritt his face was glowing—but not with cold. "What is it?" I asked, suspicious.

"I found something—two somethings, but I did not want that woman to see."

I could understand that. "What?"

He fumbled beneath the bearskin and pushed the somethings into my hands. My fingers ran over them. One was a leather bag and the other a bundle of papers. "Ohhh," I breathed out. "Where did Squint-eyed Harmen get so much money?" It was a hefty leather bag with objects round and hard inside. I was certain it would clink if I held it up and shook it. The second object crinkled under my fingers. I slid out the top paper from the bundle and held it up to the light for a moment, long enough to read the address of a letter. The wax seal was broken. I took care to unfold it beneath the bearskin and to pull it out, holding it to read with firm if frozen fingers.

"Do you know an Elsje Jansen?" At Gerritt's nod I directed him to take us to the lady's home. "And you keep the husband occupied while I talk to the wife."

We drove up to the Jansen's respectable step-roofed home inside the Albany gates. Other callers were just leaving. We were invited in with every degree of hospitality. I accepted a glass of milk punch while

Gerritt placed his thick arm around our host's shoulder and dragged him away for something less delicate. Resisting Gerritt's strong arm or his good humor was impossible, as Jans Jansen discovered.

I moved to the chair next to Elsje. "I bring some news...." I paused. Elsje looked at me with mild interest. I was known to her only as Gerritt's English friend. I am a New English woman, residing as I do in Boston, but I had good friends in the Albany colony.

"Squint-eyed Harmen is dead." I made the announcement in a neutral voice.

Her expression remained one of polite interest, yet I thought I saw a flash of relief in her eyes; perhaps it was only a slight relaxation in the lids. "He was murdered." I watched for her reaction. "We found his body," I added when she showed no signs of emotion.

"Oh, poor man," she said. "That must have been frightful for you." She leaned slightly forward in her chair, reaching out with a light touch upon my arm.

"It was," I said, thinking of frozen droplets of blood on the frigid body. "We went through his goods and found some letters...."

Elsje clenched her hands in her lap at this news. She wore a gay, multi-colored skirt, her hands were stark white in contrast to the material.

"Let us not beat about the bush," I went on. "Harmen also had a bag of money on him. Now, where could that lazy fellow come about such an amount of coins? Your name was on those letters—he

A Merry Slay Ride

was blackmailing you with them."

The lady's eyes became misty.

Don't worry," I added quickly, fearing she would cry. Then what should I do? I'm not good with females who cry. I don't cry for my own troubles; why should others? "I will not tell your husband about your dalliance with Master Dankaerts."

Elsje stirred with unease. "You don't understand." She puffed her consonants, like Gerriett. "Jaspar and I had an understanding long before I met Jans Jansen. It was my father who would not let us post our banns. Jaspar was young and untried—he was only an apprentice with no money then, but I loved him, and still do." There was a touch of defiance in her voice. "But Jans is a good man. I did not want to hurt him. I paid the little weasel what he asked."

"Gerritt and I, we will not tell the Sheriff any of this unless it becomes necessary. He has no interest, since it was only Squint-eyed Harmen. The Sheriff prefers to believe that Harmen stabbed himself through the heart. We have to found out who murdered the poor little man, no matter if he was a thief and a scoundrel. Even such a man deserves justice. That is our English law," I explained my interest.

"Why do you tell me this?" Elsje's cheeks were scarlet now.

"I must ask you—where were you this afternoon?"

The white hands unclenched, spread up and

39

outwards to indicate the room. "I was here, greeting callers. I can give you their names, if you wish."

"Perhaps you were here, but where was Jaspar Dankaerts? He had reason to murder the man who was blackmailing his lady-love." I knew where my next call must be.

Elsje leaned forward. "Oh, but Jaspar did not care. He laughed when Harmen approached him. He told Harmen to give the letters to my husband, then I would be free. I could not laugh, though. If I am exposed in this way, I am disgraced, and my good husband made to look a fool. I did not want that to happen, and so I paid him." Elsje raised her head to meet my eyes. "I felt such disgust for that little worm, but I did not kill him."

As it turned out, Jaspar Dankaerts could not have murdered Squint-eyed Harmen. He was in a sleigh with four other gentlemen, making their own New Year's calls. Gerritt insisted that Jans Jansen knew nothing of what was happening around him. "He's a good man, but as dumb as a *moff*," Gerritt concluded. "What do we do next, Hetty?"

"There are plenty of people who wanted to murder the man. We'll have to queston them."

"But Hetty, we'll have to question the whole town!" Gerritt's voice rose in dismay.

"If that's what we have to do...." I climbed into the sled, pulling the warm robe up to my nose. The Dutchman groaned as he heaved himself up beside me.

A Merry Slay Ride

It was a cheery sight to watch as high-stepping horses, harness bells jingling, sped back and forth across the frozen river pulling gaily-painted sleighs full of fur-muffled folk. I thought it a particularly pleasant tradition, paying New Year's calls to one's friends and neighbors.

Nor was our questioning the neighbors such a daunting task. We were regaled with cups of milk punch and cakes and gossip. Word of Squint-eyed Harmen's death spread as fast as the speedy sleighs on the river. The good Dutch *vrouws* were eager to learn the details, the bloodier the better. When asked who they thought might have killed the poor man, the answers were as varied as the male population of the Albany colony. Some knew of the leather bag of coins Harmen carried, so robbery was put forth as a reason for his murder—except that the bag of coins had not been taken.

One piece of gossip engaged my attention and it concerned Harmen's landlady, Jonica Skoggins. It seems the widow had a mysterious suitor. He'd been glimpsed leaving her front door early in the morning and once she'd been spied walking in the *Clover Waytie* arm and arm with a black-caped gentleman. Widowed as she claimed, I wondered why she would keep her suitor a secret, unless perhaps he was a married man. With Squint-eyed Harmen's penchant for blackmail, I knew I had to question the woman.

I waited until the last of a string of callers left. We were seated in the best parlor where stood the pride of the Dutch wife's furnishings, the great *kas* or tall chest. "Madame Skoggins," I began, "I must ask you some questions relating to Squint-eyed Harmen."

She nodded her permission.

"Was he blackmailing you?"

Madame Skoggins gave me a hard look. "Why do you ask that?"

"There is talk about you and a married gentleman—I don't judge your behavior, please understand. I just repeat what I have heard."

The woman seemed to suppress a smile. Her lips tightened. "I appreciate your concern, but I do not believe I am consorting with a married man." She leaned back in her chair, much at her ease.

I watched her face for any sign of emotion. "Then who is the man in the black cloak?"

"How people gossip," she said with a sigh. "If you must know, he is an acquaintance who has put me in the way of a small venture in commerce."

"You conduct your commercial ventures rather early in the morning, I hear." My tone was polite but the sarcasm did not escape her.

"Sometimes it is necessary—my man travels a great distance to conduct this business." She stood, intimating with a small wave of the hand that I was dismissed, that the visit was over. As she stood, the keys at her waist jangled with a tinny sound. The keys hung from a pink ribbon. My eyes followed the ribbon as it swung back and forth from her waist.

I forced myself to stand, give a brief curtsy and collect my cloak. I met Gerritt at the door. As soon as

A Merry Slay Ride

we crossed the steps into the crisp cold, I turned and muttered into my companion's ear. "Something's not right here. We've got to get into the widow's barn and we've got to find the man in the black cloak."

But the man in the black cloak found us.

We'd doubled back after we left the widow's house and parked behind her barn. Creeping inside, we were able to see a lone horse in a stall. The animal was contentedly munching on a fresh fork-full of hay. I knew it was fresh because of its sweetish smell. The animal's shaggy brown mane was dry to the touch. I gave the beast a pat and moved around it. The next stall held a high-backed sleigh covered over in canvas secured with stout ropes.

"Untie a corner, Gerritt," I directed. "Let's see what's underneath."

Gerritt obliged and pulled back a corner of canvas as I peaked over his shoulder. The sled was filled with kegs and bundles wrapped in canvas, from which bundles protruded the butts of muskets. Gerritt tipped one of the kegs. It made a distinct sloshing sound. "Rum," he said. He pushed another, smaller keg. It made no noise. He took out his knife, looking at me for instructions. I nodded, so he pried out the bung and peered down inside. He sniffed. "Black powder," he said.

We both knew the sleigh was loaded with trade goods meant for the Indians, trade goods that were prohibited under English law. The English had no wish to deal with drunken, armed savages. I glanced up in time to spot the black-caped gentleman as he rose up behind Gerritt. He was ready to whack the Dutchman with a thick pole.

"Look out!" I yelled. I threw myself under the sleigh.

I heard a thud, a grunt, a groan and another thud. I saw a tangle of boots. I meant to crawl out the other side of the sled and run for help but two bodies landed with a thud upon the barn floor and I noted the thick body of the Dutchman was on top. I deemed it prudent to wait.

"Get ropes!" Gerritt puffed out the order.

Since we were in a barn well supplied with ropes of all thicknesses, I grabbed a coil and knelt beneath the sled, passing the rope through to the Dutchman. In no time he had the black-caped man trussed up like a roasting goose.

"There, the Sheriff can't ignore this," he puffed. "Run and get him, Hetty, while I stay with the prisoner."

"The Sheriff? I don't trust the sheriff. I'm going next door to the fort. The Colonel won't be too happy to learn about the smuggling going on under his nose," I said.

Gerritt and I saw the trussed goose safe into the hands of the English soldiers. We accompanied the English lieutenant into the house. The widow Skoggins refused any knowledge of the black-caped gentleman's smuggling ventures. He was only a boarder, she claimed, and was she expected to know the movements of every one of her boarders at all hours wherever they may be? When I taxed her with her own words, that she'd used the gentleman for some business ventures, she explained to the English officer that she'd only asked him to procure a few small gifts of the natives, such as quill-decorated boots and pendants of bone and leather and such like adornments, which she gave out to friends. She knew nothing of illegal trade.

The Lieutenant was disposed to let the woman off, as he had no proof of her involvement. When I heard that, I was furious. Before he could leave her parlor, I stood up and moved next to the widow. While she smiled her thanks to the gentleman I reached out and grabbed the pink ribbon, pulling it so hard it ripped away the fabric of her apron. The keys clanked into my hand.

She gave a cry. "Give them to me! Those are my house keys."

"House keys? Let's see what they open," I jeered. I held them up in a taunting manner, just out of her reach. The widow glared at me. "Lieutenant, please have your men search Madame's bed chamber, and be sure to look into the cupboards and under the bed. I suggest they search the prisoner's room, as well."

The soldiers left at their officer's bidding. We waited in the parlor. It did not take long for the men to return with two boxes, at sight of which the widow began to sob.

"Those boxes are mine! It's all mine!"

I couldn't blame her for claiming the contents;

I'd have liked to claim two boxes full of gold and Spanish coins. "Pretty savings for a poor widow who takes in boarders. And you still know nothing of the smuggling goods in your barn? Why, that load will fill another of your boxes with gold," I said.

"I will give you a receipt for the boxes," the lieutenant said to the widow, his manner become a trifle stiff. "We'll keep them safe at the fort. I've stationed a guard in the barn, and I'll give you a receipt for the contents of the sled as soon as they've been inventoried. One of these boxes should cover the fine for illegal smuggling," he added, his mouth twisted in a wry grimace.

The widow sank into a chair, a handkerchief covering a mouth full of sobs. Tears ran down her cheeks. I waited until the lieutenant left the room before I taxed her with the murder of Squint-eyed Harmen.

"Harmen wouldn't have gotten into the sleigh with the black-caped man. He wouldn't have trusted him. You, on the other hand.... He shouldn't have trusted you, either. You might as well confess," I said. "You've not much else to lose. He was blackmailing you, wasn't he?"

The widow nodded as she continued to sob. "It was worth than that," she managed to say. Her shoulders shook beneath her black woolen dress.

I wondered what could be worse than blackmail, but when the widow confided what Squint-eyed Harmen required, I tended to agree with her.

46

A Merry Slay Ride

"He wanted me to marry him or he would tell the sheriff," she said, speaking through her tears. "I laughed at that, because I paid off the sheriff to turn the blind eye to our dealings. But then he threatened to tell the English officers. You see how I could not let him do that, and I could not bring myself to marry him! All he wanted was a life where he could be lazy and live on my money. He could have it all, all my goods, and not lift a finger. Well, that's what he thought. I could not let him." She lifted the kerchief from her face at that, looking up at me.

"I could not let him," she said, repeating herself. "I agreed to pay New Year's calls with him because he pressed me so, that we would tell my friends that we were engaged now. My friends... why, what would they think of me? Such a little worm...." Her eyes were dark and stormy through the tears that continued to fall. "I took with me a knife from the kitchen and I stabbed him! Then I jumped out of the sleigh and let it go where it would. I didn't care. I don't care." She shook her head in defiance.

I fell back in my own chair. The guard stood rigid by the door. He'd heard it all. I waited until the lieutenant came back into the room before I spoke in a firm voice.

"You had to protect yourself—he threatened you with bodily harm." (Well, thought I, any woman would regard marriage with Squint-eyed Harmen as bodily harm.) I turned to the lieutenant. "This woman acted in self-defense. The dead man provoked her into striking or she would lose her honor." Let the courts decide, I thought. An Albany jury would be apt to agree.

And so the jury did agree. With my hint for her defense, the widow Skoggins was saved from the hangman. Not that she did not pay a high price for her act. She was shunned by friends, neighbors and the English boarders, for so Anneke and Gerritt informed me upon my next visit. Losing her livelihood or her reputation did not break her spirit, but losing her gold did. The fine she paid for smuggling ate up one box of her gold; the other went with her court case. The cost of slaying is prohibitive.

Copyright © 2008 M. E. Kemp

On the Sixth Night of Hanukah

Helen Schwartz

Friday night, two days after Christmas, I drove into the parking lot of Temple Beth Shalom, off duty, but with my Glock in a shoulder holster. At the rabbi's request.

A powdering of snow covered the cars already parked for the dinner before services. This year, *Shabbat*—the Jewish Sabbath—fell on the sixth night of Hanukah, and families came to create memories of the eight-day Festival of Lights. Jews held to Hanukah against the flood of Christmas good cheer so attractive to their children. Before my ex-wife moved with our daughter to St. Louis, I'd brought Terry to Hanukah services at the Temple.

I parked near the back, where the skull and crossbones had been spray-painted on the wall of the education wing, then squatted in front of the graffiti trying to figure out its meaning.

Billy Small, the captain of the police department's bomb unit, walked up. "Hello, Bryant. You on duty?"

"Nope. The rabbi asked me to stay overnight, to back up the security guard, at least while the Temple's hosting a bunch of homeless families."

"The Hospitality Network. I didn't know before that any Jewish groups were involved."

"Yeah. Beth Shalom's the only temple, so we usually take Christmas and Easter weeks when things are quieter here than at the churches."

"Whattaya make of it?" The captain gestured toward the skull and crossbones.

"Probably not terrorists—foreign or homegrown. There's no writing—nothing about Jews or Israel, nothing in Arabic." Synagogues and Jewish schools had been bombed in France, Turkey, and Tunisia since September 11, 2001. In the United States, threats and attacks against Jewish schools, cemeteries and temples had cropped up from New Jersey to California. The Temple had beefed up its security system and hired a guard for special events and weekends—Friday night services, Saturday when most Bar and Bat Mitzvahs were celebrated, and Sunday school classes.

"Why not homegrown? You know this part of the Midwest still has a Klan presence." Small blew warmth on his ungloved hands.

"Message not clear. Is this place supposed to be poison or is it a death threat? Anti-semites aren't subtle. Either the drawings are Nazi swastikas or they show hanging or bombs." I looked at Small. No reaction. "This looks like amateur hour to me. Maybe some neighborhood kids. Could be against the Temple. Could be against the homeless." I zipped up my leather jacket. "I'm going in now to check with the agency liaison, Joan Marin."

"We'll have a couple of cars around for the usual traffic control. After the parking lot clears, squad cars will check during the night."

On the Sixth Night of Hanukah

We shook hands and I walked around to the front, testing doors as I went, near the school and side entrances. Only the front door was open. I introduced myself to the security guard and found out where the homeless guests were having dinner since I knew the congregational Hanukah party would be in the community room.

I hadn't been very active in the Temple since my divorce two years ago but I'd volunteered a couple times for the Hospitality Network. That's when I met Joan, the social worker from the Temple who trained the volunteers and worked with the families during the day. On Sundays, I'd helped set up cots to turn Temple classrooms into bedrooms, one per family, plus two for the congregation's Overnight Hosts. Each night a new crew of volunteers served as Dinner Hosts, another group hosted breakfast and put out supplies for the families to make bag lunches. Busses picked the families up daily and took them to the social agency. The parents worked on finding a job and a place to stay. At 6:00 p.m. back to the Temple. The next Sunday the families moved on to their next week-long stay. I couldn't imagine being desperate enough to live under those conditions.

In the Youth Lounge, red-checkered tablecloths covered four bridge-sized tables, with families and hosts seated at three of them. A wet bar held heated steel pans of home-made barbecued chicken, green beans and Tater Tots plus little bowls of applesauce and a platter of giant oatmeal-raisin cookies.

One young woman, cocoa-colored with a dark-skinned baby on her hip, complained to the grandmotherly Dinner Host at her table. "I ast you all three times to take that crib outta my room. And it's still there today. This baby used to sleeping with me."

Joan Marin swept past me and confronted the teen-aged mother. "We're leaving the crib in your room. It's not safe for a ten-month old like Precious to sleep in your cot. What if you roll over on her in the night? Those are our rules, and you agreed to follow them."

"Would you like some apple juice for your baby?" The grandmotherly congregant got up to fetch it, attracting the sullen mother's attention and freeing Joan to bring me up to speed.

Joan wore a striped t-shirt and jeans. Her reddish-gold, slightly kinky hair stood up and out, controlled only by a large toothed clip in back. I figured Joan was in her mid-thirties, not bad looking, even though she didn't bother with makeup. Joan dumped her hobo handbag behind the wet bar and pulled out the logbook, knowing I'd want a rundown of any problems during the week.

I loaded a plate with Tater Tots, added a chicken leg and stood with my back to the bar, like the new gunfighter in town sizing up the crowd. I didn't feel like John Wayne. "How do they stand it," I asked.

"It's pretty grim, but it's short term. These folks aren't chronic homeless, they just need some breathing space to re-establish themselves." Joan pointed with her chin at a family group at the far table. "Bill

On the Sixth Night of Hanukah

Thornton lost his main job, but they could hang on until he got laid off as night watchman. They just lost their home."

I took the family in at a glance. A scrawny blond man in his 30's in a white t-shirt and jeans sat next to a woman who looked older than him, dark hair drawn back in a bun, with three school kids sitting quiet, the oldest a sullen-looking boy about twelve. They sat in silence, eating but with no sign of enjoyment.

"I've never seen a man with any of the families before. I thought they were trouble." I crunched on a Tater Tot.

"They can be, but we don't want to break up intact families. Two wage earners give the family a better chance than one." Joan opened the log and started her briefing. "It's been a crazy week, not even counting Christmas." She opened a diet Coke and pointed in the logbook. "Monday night the fire alarm went off around ten waking everyone. Fire Captain thought someone was smoking in one of the 'bedrooms' and that set off the alarm. Some smoke smell in the Thorntons' bedroom."

I looked back at Thornton. He caught me staring at him as his daughter nagged at him. She started pulling his sleeve and he pulled his hand back, as though to smack her. She ducked and fell silent. Then he opened her waxed carton of milk.

Joan, checking the log, missed the incident. "Christmas day, almost everyone got picked up to spend the holiday with relatives, but one of the families—mother and two pre-schoolers—hasn't returned from her sister's." Her brow wrinkled as she paused. "There's an abusive ex-boyfriend she's mentioned. We haven't been able to get in touch with them at the address she left."

"You worried?"

Joan pressed her lips together. "I think the sister's move was skipping out on the rent, not fear of violence. Anyway, that's the agency's problem. I don't see a danger to the Temple and the rest of the guests."

I nodded. If the boyfriend had attacked during Christmas, no reason to leave graffiti on the Temple yesterday. "Was anyone around Christmas Day?"

"The Office closed," she said. "A security guard was on duty. One family from the Hospitality Network stayed in the Temple, and a couple of members took them out to dinner. No sense getting a whole bunch of volunteers going for one family." Joan raised her head and pointed her chin toward the nearest table where a dark-skinned, tired-looking woman tried to feed a sickly child as her antsy nine-year old kept me under surveillance. The little girl's hair had been divided into squares, with a little pig-tail in the center of each, fastened by a pink barrette. She looked up at us with a bold shyness.

"Hello, Tameeka. How's your brother?" Joan said, then turned to me. "Tameeka's mother took her little brother to the emergency room last night with a high fever." She shut the logbook and put it away.

"He's okay today," the little girl said without

On the Sixth Night of Hanukah

much conviction. "Are you a policeman?" She flashed me a smile.

Joan jumped in. "Meet Detective Bryant."

Tameeka got up, walked over. "Pleased to meet you." She shook my hand. "I want to be a police officer when I grow up."

Joan laughed. "Don't count on it, David. Yesterday, one of the Overnight Hosts was an attorney and this morning she wanted to be a lawyer when she grows up."

Tameeka placed her hands on her hips and cocked her head at the social worker, but her smiling pout showed she took Joan's no-nonsense humor in stride.

"You going to the dinner in the Community Room," Joan asked.

"Hadn't planned to, but I'm not on duty here til eight," I said.

"Let's crash and see if there's any potato *latkes* left."

"Sure," I said. My mouth started to water and I tossed the rest of my cookie into the waste bin behind the counter.

"What's a lat-key," Tameeka asked. "Can I go, too? I've never seen a Jewish Christmas party." Her mother started to grab for her, recognized she'd have to get up and settled for a glare that spoke her disapproval.

Joan looked at me, then at the exhausted woman. "Would it be okay if we took Tameeka with us, Mrs.

Brown. I'll get her back by 8 o'clock, and if you're asleep I'll make sure she brushes her teeth."

Tameeka's mother smiled. "Thank you, Ms. Marin." Her son reached out his spoon and started pounding on the table. She turned to Tameeka. "You mind Ms. Marin, you hear?"

The little girl jumped up and down, tucked herself between Joan and me, taking our hands as we headed for the community room.

"Do you know the story of Hanukah," I asked, waiting for Tameeka to shake her head. "It has nothing to do with Christmas, you know." Who was I kidding? Like all Jewish parents I'd had the difficult job of telling my daughter that Christmas was nice for Christians, but we were Jews and we celebrated Hanukah.

"A long time ago...."—out came the story-telling voice—"a wicked ruler conquered Israel and spoiled the special Temple in Jerusalem, by setting up false idols for the Jews to worship. The people revolted and drove out the bad guys. When the Temple priests restored order, all the holy oil was ruined except for one bottle, enough to keep the Eternal Light lit for only one day. It would take eight days to get a new batch of holy oil. But a miracle occurred and the one little bottle lasted for eight days. That's why we light a candle each night for eight nights."

"I like the story about baby Jesus better," Tameeka said.

Smart kid, I thought. That's why we'd made sure

On the Sixth Night of Hanukah

to give our daughter Terry a gift each night of Hanukah, a feeble attempt to counteract a month of Christmas carols everywhere and manger scenes and Santa Claus. Christmas was a seduction, not an attack. No one came to the Temple and turned off the Eternal Light (now electric); no one forced us to deck the halls with boughs of holly. I remembered my teen years when I wouldn't say any part of the Temple services that I didn't believe in one hundred per cent. In high school assembly, I enjoyed singing Christmas carols, but when we got to the chorus—"Christ the Savior is born!"—I mouthed the words. No sound came from my lips. I'd been taught Jesus was a good and holy man, but Jews didn't believe Jesus was the Messiah, the Savior.

Tameeka and I found two seats free at one of the ten large tables and pulled up another chair. Joan scoped out the *latke* situation at the buffet, gave a thumbs-up and signaled Tameeka to come. Barrettes bobbing, she almost ran to the buffet.

At each white-clothed table a special Hanukah menorah twinkled with a rainbow of candles. On the first night, we'd lit one candle. Tonight on the sixth night, six of the eight candleholders held burning lights, plus another candle off to the side—the *shamos* —used to light the others.

Joan arrived with plates full of the crispy potato pancakes. Tameeka carefully held one small bowl with applesauce and another with sour cream.

Her pink barrettes swished as she watched me, then Joan, load up our *latkes* with more calories. Joan cut off a big piece and offered the fork to Tameeka. She was busy making her own lat-key by the time the singing started:

Dreydl, dreydl, dreydl.

I made it out of clay

And when it's dry and ready

Then *dreydl* I will play.

I picked up one of the little plastic toys in the center of the table. "*Dreydl*," I said, and started the four-sided top spinning to Tameeka's delight.

"Let's play," said Ethan, the boy her age sitting next to her.

I showed her that each side of the *dreydl* had a different Hebrew letter, and Ethan explained the rules of the game—what happened if each of the letters lay face up after the spin. Then he pulled the chocolate coins wrapped in gold foil from the center and passed them out to Joan, me, Tameeka and himself.

"Hanukah *gelt*," I said. "*Gelt* means money. But this is the kind you can eat."

The game began with the advantage passed back and forth between the two children until I got lucky and won the pot. Both children looked at me in outrage that an adult had played to win, but they kept quiet as I raked in the pile of candy.

The rabbi stood to announce that services were about to start. The crowd started to leave, and I split my take between the two children, to loud cheers.

"How did you like your first Hanukah party," I

asked Tameeka.

"Can I take the Hanukah stuff_people left on the tables?"

"Just what you can carry in your hands," Joan said.

Tameeka emptied the current contents of her hands into her pockets. "Ok," she said, sweeping each table, but sticking to the rules Joan had set.

"I'm checking in with security before I go back to the hosting area," I said.

"Okay, I'll see that Tameeka gets settled before I leave for the night."

"Thanks for coming by, Joan." For the first time I felt awkward, very aware of Tameeka's presence. Duh, I thought. Who was I to thank Joan? She ran the whole operation. My job was to reassure the two female Overnight Hosts—a middle-aged English professor and a young attorney new to the area.

Joan looked up at me, then turned to keep the pink-barrettes in sight as Tameeka finished her sweep.

"I'll call you tomorrow," I said. "To let you know what happens." And then we separated, my steps heading for the entrance.

* * *

By eleven o'clock, not a creature was stirring. The security guard stayed at the front entrance, with an occasional walk around the outside. I'd checked in with the Overnight Hosts and made sure all the guest families were in their rooms and had their doors locked. I dragged a comfortable armchair over to the alarmed door nearest the temporary bedrooms and pulled a paperback thriller out of my jacket.

I must've dozed off. Loud knocks on the glass door woke me up. A short black woman with a huge Santa-sized plastic zip bag over her shoulder rattled the push bar with two solemn, little kids standing by. A renewed snowfall had already dusted them with white.

"Come around the front," I yelled, pointing to the main entrance. She nodded and started to trudge.

I called Joan on my cell phone as I headed toward the front. "I think the missing family just showed up."

She gave me their names. "Their room's still made up. Tell her I'll be by to sort things out tomorrow morning."

The security guard, finished with his outside rounds, had opened the door for the family by the time I got there.

"We're back," the mother said as she knelt to pull down the hoods on the slightly too-big parkas her sons were wearing. Snowflakes in her cornrows were melting, glittering in the lights.

Just then the older Overnight Host scuffed in with the Directions folder clutched to her purple flannel bathrobe. She took charge, insisting on seeing identification and calling Joan to confirm arrangements. Professor Hirschberg then ordered us to our respective duties, staying behind to reset the security alarm with the aid of the Directions. Twenty minutes later, order restored, I picked up my thriller.

On the Sixth Night of Hanukah

When I woke up, the lights were off, with only the red EXIT sign giving a feeble light. Silence. What had waked me? I stayed unmoving in my chair, except for the creep of my right hand toward my shoulder holster.

Then swearing and a hopping motion caught the sensors' attention and turned on the lights. Bill Thornton cursed, twisted and fell to the floor. He lifted himself and pulled a small blue *dreydl* from beneath him. I swept aside the rainbow scatter of tiny tops on the floor near the door and held out my hand to Thornton, but he stood on his own. I took the *dreydl* from him, noticing the smell of cigarette smoke on his clothes.

The Professor in Purple shuffled in as fast as her scuffs allowed, clutching the Directions manual. Tameeka in her pajamas peeked around her.

"Thought I heard something," Thornton said. "That alarm system." He pointed to a box just above eye level to the right of the door with more blinking lights than I remembered from earlier in the evening. "I was a night watchman. Blinking means it's not armed."

So the door had been open for several hours and Thornton figured he could grab a smoke. An infraction of the rules, but Joan could take care of it tomorrow.

"Could I check with your Directions manual, Professor?" Looking a bit sheepish, she handed it over and exited. Tameeka had disappeared.

61

As Thornton turned to go, I noticed a streak of black on his cheek and a bulge in the side of his Pacers jacket.

"What've you got there?" I patted down his jacket over the bulge.

Thornton pulled away. "Leave me be. Me and my family're getting out of this Jew hellhole. Right now."

I held on to him. In the struggle, an aerosol can fell from his jacket. I turned it with my foot to see the label—black spray paint. I snapped cuffs onto Thornton, glad his family wasn't around to see his arrest. I called into the station, requesting a squad car and told them to put me on active duty.

The security guard came back to check out the noise.

"The alarms aren't armed. Keep an eye on him." I nodded toward Thornton, now standing with his back to the door. I picked up the spray can, bagged it, and labeled it.

A police car pulled silently into the parking lot with its lights flashing.

"I know how to arm it," the security guard said, pointing his head to the panel of lights. "Sorry I didn't catch it earlier."

Where was the police officer? He must've taken a look around, especially out back. Then I saw two figures approaching. Since the door was unarmed, I pushed it open. No alarm.

"Look what I found in the parking lot." An

On the Sixth Night of Hanukah

officer pushed Thornton's older son in before him. "Is he one of your 'guests'? He was near the graffiti and someone's added a Klan sign."

The boy's face impassive, he avoided looking at his father and stuffed his fists into the pockets of his jeans, a black smear on his right hand. Some black paint streaked up his jacket, across his cheek and into his hair—as though someone had interrupted him while he was spraying.

"His father had the can of paint when he came in," I said, "and some paint on his cheek."

Twenty minutes later, things were quiet once more. I'd called Joan and she talked on the phone with Mrs. Thornton. The patrol officers took Thornton and his son to the station, but the rest of the family stayed on, at least until the police and the agency could sort everything out tomorrow. The Security Guard armed the alarm system, and I returned the Directions with an update to Professor Hirschberg.

Case solved. I could go to the station and write up a report. But first I picked up all the *dreydls* I'd swept to the side.

A pig-tailed head, minus pink barrettes, peeked around the corner from the classroom hall. "I saw him go out," Tameeka said.

"For a smoke," I said, putting the *dreydls* in my jacket pocket. "While I was asleep."

She nodded.

"You should have got me up, Tameeka. As long as the alarm system was off, someone could leave or break in without anyone knowing. Police work in teams, you know."

Tameeka avoided looking at me. I walked her back to her family's room.

I put my hand under her head and raised it toward me. "You set a clever trap with the *dreydls*, Tameeka. I hereby award you the Order of the *Dreydl* for bravery and smarts." I dropped the blue *dreydl* into her hand. "Now get some sleep, young woman."

She turned the knob with the quiet skill of a cat burglar and smiled up at me. "Happy Hanukah, Detective Bryant."

"Happy New Year, Tameeka." I vowed to myself that I'd keep track of this little girl and her family. Never too early to start recruiting.

Copyright © 2008 Helen Schwartz

Something Extra for Christmas

Radine Trees Nehring

The door closed behind them. *Ka-chunk.*

Henry put his suitcase down, glanced at Carrie, and said, "Well." He cleared his throat. "Well, here we are, an old married couple home from the honeymoon."

Carrie, who had been just as frozen in awkwardness as her new husband, said "Pfmmmpf—hunh-hunh," before real giggles burst out. In a flash they were both laughing, extending their arms, hugging until the noise faded away. She hadn't a clue to what was so funny and doubted Henry did either.

"Well," he said again. "What next?" Shall I put these bags in your... our... bedroom?"

Carrie took off her coat, ran fingers through white curls, and said "Christmas! Oh, golly, I need to get started on Christmas right this minute. The wedding put me way behind. I will never marry you at Thanksgiving again, Henry King." Another giggle burst out, faded.

"But, since you're here to help me, I can make it. Drop our bags in the bedroom, then we'll bring all the Christmas things up from the basement. Do you have any decorations stored in your boxes in my... our garage?"

He shook his head. "Irena hired out seasonal decorating and this humble cop wasn't invited to participate. I don't think we had any decorations of our own. Anyway, the money was hers, so she had the say about everything, including Christmas." He paused. "About all I really owned was my clothes, a few tools, books, my fishing stuff. And that's what I took with me when we divorced."

Carrie's next words sounded too sharp in her ears, and her eyes felt wet behind the gold-rimmed glasses. "Ah, never mind. With half my worldly goods I thee endow, and I sure have enough Christmas decorations to go around." She reached up to stroke the tuft of grey hair above his left ear. "That means half the chores, too. The decorating will probably take us part of today and most of tomorrow. Later this week we'll start our Christmas shopping. But for now, on to the basement, husband dear."

* * *

"Last load!" He sat down in his new recliner and contemplated the stack of boxes in the center of the room. "Do you put all this stuff up every year?"

"You bet. If I left anything out Rob would notice. Most of these decorations have been around since he was a baby. But, believe me, if that man ever gets married, I'm going to send most of them home with him."

She bent to open a box, and lifted out a bronze candelabra. "Not this though. I'm keeping this."

"Carrie, isn't that..."

"A menorah. Yes. Sylvia Margolis gave it to me at least thirty-five years ago. We worked together at the library, and she was my best friend back then. We often discussed religion. I learned a lot about Judaism from her."

"So you use this as a Christmas decoration?"

"Not really. Chanukah does fall in December, though how close it is to Christmas depends on the Jewish calendar for that year. It's an eight-day celebration, honoring a one-day supply of lamp oil that miraculously lasted eight days. That happened during the Maccabean War of 167 B.C.E. when the Jews took their Temple in Jerusalem back from the Syrians, and re-lit the Temple's eternal flame. A new oil supply didn't reach the Temple until the ninth day. See, there are eight candles here. The ninth one that's set apart is a service candle called the *shamos*. It's lit first, then is used to light the other eight. A new candle is added each night until all are burning together on the final night."

"So… do you do it like that?"

"Yes, most years. The way I observe it is peaceful, very unlike the sometimes noisy and overly-elaborate celebration of Christmas. Sylvia gave me verses to read and think about each night as I light candles. Some are quite familiar since they're in our Old Testament, too. A few of the verses are like what's sung in Handel's Messiah."

"Such as…?"

"Oh, um, 'Arise, shine, for your light has come, and the splendor of the Lord shall dawn upon you.' My favorite verse is 'The Lord is my light and my help; whom shall I fear?'"

"I like that."

"Yes." She paused, then lifted the lid of a large box. "Okay, time to get going. First, let's decorate the tree. It's made in sections, so we need to put it together. But before we start, I'll make cocoa. That's part of tradition, too."

* * *

Carrie looked through the mall crowds and spied a gloriously empty bench. She bent over and, leading with her head, pushed between a woman carrying two huge shopping bags and a boy who's ragged jeans would surely fall off at any moment. Kids!

Henry—a head taller than either the encumbered woman or the boy—followed along easily while people glanced at him, then hurried out of his way. He joined Carrie, and the two of them sat, saying nothing, while crowd noises swirled around them, Santa ho-ho'd from his throne across the mall concourse, and Deck the Halls changed to Jingle Bells. The boy in drooping pants stopped walking and leaned against the wall, staring at Santa.

Henry said, "That kid sure looks glum." He moved a large sack from his lap to the bench seat. "Kids these days specialize in looking glum. Still... at Christmas...."

"Well, Rob McCrite never looked glum," Carrie said, "and his jeans sure didn't droop. But I'm thinking back at least twenty years. What age do you think that kid is? Maybe twelve or thirteen?"

"About that."

"I feel like hugging him" Carrie said. "He's probably wishing he was young enough to climb in

Santa's lap."

They sat in silence again, letting voices, carols, and "Ho-ho" fill the air space. Finally Henry asked, "Should I take this load to the car before we continue? Or are we done?"

Carrie came back from her private thoughts, looked away from the glum boy, and reached for her list. "Let's see." She read names aloud. "That's it, I think. We'll do gift certificates for the mail carrier and the couple who delivers our newspaper. Anyone else… maybe friends of yours?"

"No one," he said.

"We're done, then."

"Not quite, my love. There's us."

"Oh, yes, but we'll do that later. We need to shop alone."

"There's not much time left. Why not now? We drove thirty miles to get to this mall. How about you pick a store where you want me to shop and I'll pick one for you. Then we'll split up."

"That's a great idea. We can begin a McCrite and King Christmas tradition. Picking stores. I like it."

"How about I take this load of stuff to the car before I shop? I'll pick that store across the mall for me. The Outdoor Store. Now you tell me where to shop."

"How about Gem Boutique?"

"Not Kitchen Corner?"

"Don't you dare!" She glanced up at him and saw the grin.

"Okay, Ms. McCrite. Meet you back here in, what? Thirty minutes?"

"Give me an hour. We can meet at this bench. The one who has to wait will have fun watching Santa and the kids."

Henry hoisted packages and disappeared in the crowd. Carrie headed for the Outdoor Store.

She was at the store's entrance when a loud bang sounded behind her. Then, before she understood what she'd heard, there was a second bang and a crack from somewhere over her head, followed by screams. The shouts of one woman grew louder than every other noise. "Tommyeeee. My baby. Tommy, Tommyeee!" As Carrie turned, she saw the woman on her knees in front of Santa's throne, wailing inarticulately.

No! Those were gunshots.

Carrie looked toward Santa's platform, trying to make sense of what was happening. People ran, some crouched, every one of them seemed to be shrieking. Santa lay crumpled on the floor. On Santa's throne—his dark form outlined against the snow scene painted on the wall behind him—sat the glum boy. His left arm circled a toddler with a bloody cheek. His right hand held a gun against the child's head.

Oh, merciful God, oh, Prince of Peace... a child... two children. Dear God. A mere baby....

She imagined Henry's voice inside her head: "Stay away. Extreme danger. Erratic shooter. You could end up dead at any second. Danger... danger...

danger. Let the law handle this."

He's barely a toddler. Probably not two yet. He hasn't a clue what coming to see Santa means.

People continued scattering, crawling, shouting into cell phones. Feeling like an automaton, Carrie walked toward the tableau—-a mother, a boy, and a baby.

"Stay back," the boy shouted. If anyone comes close, I'm gonna put a bullet in this kid."

Only a baby. His little blue overalls have spots of blood on them.

"Hello," Carrie said to the boy with the gun.

The Lord is my light and my help; whom shall I fear? Whom shall I fear?!

"He's just a baby," she said to the boy. "If you give him to his mother, I will come and sit with you. You don't need a little kid." She thought of Henry's grandson Johnny, about the age of this baby with a smear of blood on his cheek. He wasn't making a sound, but he was conscious. His eyes were wide open. Could babies go into shock?

"No! Stay AWAY!"

"I'd like to talk with you."

"Why? Heard enough talk."

"I want you to tell me your story. Tell me why you're sitting in Santa's chair holding a baby."

"Because... because... then they can't make me."

"No, they can't," she said. *Oh God, give me the right things to say. Tell me what is behind this tragedy.*

The toddler's mother lay on the floor, sobbing.

"I will listen to your story," Carrie said. "I need to understand why people want to make you do something you don't like."

"Like? I HATE it. I hate him."

"Him?"

"My dad." The boy almost spit the words.

"Tell me. I can help."

But how? The offer of help had come unbidden.

"I need to know how to help you, and only you can tell me that. First, will you hand me that baby? A baby is no good to you. He can't understand anything. I can. I can listen to you."

The gun was still against the toddler's head.

"Don't come closer."

Careful, careful. He's so angry.

"I'm not moving. I won't come closer unless you tell me it's okay."

Carrie didn't look around, but she was now aware of silence in the mall. The carols, even the mother's crying, had stopped. All she could hear was her own thumping heart, and then, in the background, the easily recognizable creak of a police officer's equipment belt. *No, no, give me time. Let me get the baby away from him. Let me help both of these children.*

The people who walked in darkness have seen a great light.

Where was Henry? Still at the car, she hoped. He had been a cop for all those years before she met him. He might....

"Son, let me take the baby and give him to his mother. I will stay with you instead."

Suddenly the boy laughed, and the anguish in his laughter brought tears to Carrie's eyes. "Son," he shouted. "Not a son. They took my mom. Now I'm a nobody."

"You are definitely somebody. You are definitely God's child, and God loves you right now."

Am I saying the right thing? God, help me.

Santa stirred, then lifted his head to look around. Carrie didn't see any blood—maybe he was okay. That was a reason for gratitude. "Santa," she said, almost shouting, hoping all could hear. "Do not bother the boy in your chair. He is in charge now. Leave him alone."

The boy stood, his arm still around the toddler. "Nobody move!" he shouted.

"Nobody's moving," Carrie said.

Silence.

"May I come closer now? If you give me the child I will hand him to his mother, then I will sit by you. I promise. I want to hear your story."

"Not a story. It's true."

He was waving the gun, possibly pointing it at first one target behind her, then another, but, for the moment, he wasn't pointing the gun at her. She didn't dare look around, but could feel tension vibrating, filling the mall concourse.

"Son, give me the baby, let his mother take him."

"Mother?" Tears now glistened in the boy's eyes.

Tears? Maybe this was a second reason for gratitude. She took a step forward, and could see that the crying eyes were blue. The boy's hair was dirty blond.

"I am a mother, too. I have a son like you. His name is Rob. Now, why don't you give me that boy so his mother can take him away. You don't need him." She took a few more small sliding steps toward Santa's platform, letting her toes tell her when she reached the edge.

Moving so quickly that Carrie jerked in fright, the boy shoved the baby into her arms, then pointed the gun at her head.

She could feel the child moving. He was breathing evenly, and it looked like all the blood had come from a deep scratch on his face. A third reason to be grateful.

As she turned toward the child's mother, Carrie glanced up and saw an almost empty mall. Almost. Henry sat alone on their bench, waiting for her. He looked so casual. What was he thinking right now?

Blessed is the Lord our God, Ruler of the universe, who performed wondrous deeds... at this season.

The mother took her son and hurried away. A woman in uniform came from behind a display in the Outdoor Store and pulled mother and child out of sight.

"Now," Carrie said, "tell me all about it." She sat on the edge of the platform and turned toward the boy. The hole in the gun barrel, so close now, looked huge. Where did this kid, barely a teenager, get a

Something Extra for Christmas

handgun?

Stupid question. Anyone can get guns these days. Even children.

Henry still had two revolvers left from being a police officer, but he kept them unloaded and locked away. He'd stopped carrying any gun after he shot and killed a boy back in Kansas City. It was in the line of duty they said. The boy had just murdered a convenience store clerk and turned the gun toward Henry.

Not long after that, Henry retired from the police force.

Justifiable, they'd told him, but he still suffered. A boy with a gun. "He was just a kid, Carrie. A young kid."

She began weeping for Henry, sitting alone on the bench behind her, waiting. She wept for that dead boy. Then she turned tear-filled eyes toward the boy who was right here, and still alive.

"Okay, I'm listening," she said, letting him see her tears.

She had to wait for him to stop crying. The gun wavered a bit but, most of the time, it pointed at her.

"They... they say I can't live with Mom. I have to go live with my dad and his new family. Just because Mom has it tough. It's not her fault! It was only a few dollars. She wanted...wanted me to have a bike for Christmas."

Carrie thought she understood. "Your mom wanted to give you a Christmas present and she...

75

stole money?"

"The woman she keeps house for is rich. Why would it matter to her? See, someone stole my old bike and I can't walk my paper route and still make it to school on time. Papers don't come early enough.

"The cops barely paid attention to us. But they sure paid attention to that rich bit… lady Mom works for. We looked for bikes at Goodwill and the Salvation Army, but there wasn't none left.

"Your mom works hard."

"Two jobs. Cleaning and cooking all day. Waitressing from four until eleven."

"Seems to me the two of you need help. Where is your mom now?"

"In jail. They called my dad, told him to come get me. He wouldn't've said yes if the cops didn't ask him. He never even gives us money when he's s'posed to. But I can take care of myself until Mom comes home. Then I can take care of her. She needs me."

And you need her.

"Well now, this shouldn't be too hard to straighten out. Do you go to any church?"

"Not now. Mom's too tired. Used to go. Lord's Chapel."

"Then you know about God. Know He loves you and your mom. You know about Jesus being born to help us live better lives. So, shall we get started doing that? Hand me the gun."

Miraculously, he did.

"Now, let's walk together to find someone who

can help you and your mom."

Then—with the assistance of an amazing number of people who felt the true Christmas spirit—that's exactly what they did.

Which was her fourth reason for gratitude.

* * *

"I was horrified when I saw what was happening," Henry said at the breakfast table three days later, when they were finally ready to talk about it. "Horrified when I saw that you had gotten involved. But I wasn't surprised. I know you too well, I guess. You tend to do stuff… and I… I… well, I thought about having hope. I couldn't think about losing you, so what I thought about was hope, and that verse you said when you lit the candles the other night. 'The Lord is my light and my help; whom shall I fear?'"

"It came out okay," Carrie said.

"Yes."

After a moment of silence, he said, "I guess you don't mind that my gift to you was a bicycle for that boy?"

"Nope. That means you got a coat and sweaters for his mother from me."

He stood, walked around the table, and pulled her up into a hug. "There's nothing I need that I don't already have," he said.

Copyright © 2008 Radine Trees Nehring

Gracie's Gift from the East

Gary R. Hoffman

The car carrying the three men rolled to a stop. The woman, who had been kicking the bumper of an old pick-up truck and calling it several nasty names, stopped and looked at them. "Can I help you?" she asked calmly.

"With all that steam coming from your engine, thought we might be able to help you," the driver said.

"I think this darned contraption was sent by the devil to torment me," she said. "It'll run fine for a month or two and then go haywire. You can see what it's doin' to me today."

"Well, ma'am, I know things like that are maddening, but maybe we can help. You live close around here?"

She cocked up an eyebrow and looked at the men. "Close enough. Don't think I've ever seen you fellers around here before."

"We're looking for a man named Jimmy Sims," the man in the backseat said. "We just didn't have any idea he lived so far out in the country." The driver glanced at him in the rear view mirror.

"Jimmy Sims," the woman said, mulling the name over in her mind. "You fellers must be lost. Don't think I've ever heard of him. Lived around these parts all my life. Name just doesn't ring any bells."

The driver spoke. "Well, since we're here and you're having trouble, how about we drive you home and find something to put water in?" The man in the passenger's seat tapped the driver's leg with the back of his hand. He pushed it away.

The woman paused for a few seconds. "I suppose. I've been in town for groceries, and they're in the seat."

"No problem," the driver said.

The woman turned her back to get her bags from the passenger's side of the pick-up. "Are you crazy?" the man in the back seat whispered hoarsely.

"She's a harmless old lady," the driver said. "Kind of reminds me of my granny. And besides, it's Christmas Eve. Wouldn't want to leave her out here now."

"Christmas, Shismas, I'm not sure about this," the passenger's seat guy said.

The driver got out, opened the trunk, and helped the woman load her bags. There were just a few. She got in the back seat. "Where to?" the driver asked.

"Go down here about a mile and the roads forks. Take the left side for another mile. I'm the only house down there."

"I'm Johnny," the driver said. "And this guy next to me is Sam. David is in the back with you."

"Folks call me Gracie."

The last mile was downhill into a valley. They passed a grove of pecan trees and the road ended at the back of the house. It was a typical farm house with porches around the entire building. It needed painting, but other than that, it was neat and the yard looked well kept even though there were still patches of snow here and there. A clear creek ran along the north side of the area. Old white oak trees surrounded the house.

"Let me help you with those bags," Johnny said.

"Thanks, I appreciate that."

Johnny set the bags on a table by the back door that looked like it had thousands of things put on it over the years. "I'd sure like to pay you fellers for your help," Gracie said, "but money is a bit tight right now."

"Don't you worry about that," Johnny said. "We're just glad we came along when we did. Right guys?" he said and looked at the other two men who were still in the car. All he received in return was some mumbles.

"Tell you what I could do," Gracie said. "I've got plenty of makin's inside for some biscuits and gravy. How about if I whip you boys up a batch?"

David stepped from the back seat. "Boy, that does sound good. I haven't had a home cooked meal in ages."

"Well, it's settled then," she said. "Come on in, and I'll get some coffee started."

The kitchen looked like something "city" people paid thousands of dollars to get done to their new houses. "You still use that hand pump by the sink?" Sam asked.

She laughed. "Oh, it's still hooked up, but I seldom use it. I mainly just keep it there to remind me of how things used to be. And I never could get Willy to take it out."

"Willy?"

"My husband, God rest his soul. He passed away four years come next week. I guess I was lucky. I had him for fifty seven years."

"You were married for fifty seven years?" Sam asked.

"Yep. Been tryin' to run this place on my own since then."

"Can't you sell it?" Johnny asked.

"Oh, in a heartbeat, but don't have any plans of that." She now had a table full of flour and was mixing lard in with it. The oven was already on.

"Not tryin' to be nasty, ma'am, but I'd think that would be pretty hard for a woman of your age to do," David said.

She laughed. "Just getting' out of bed in the morning is hard for a woman of my age, too." She shook a rolling pin at him. "And don't go askin' how old. That's not a polite thing to do to a woman at any age."

David chuckled. "Yes, ma'am. Understood." She started rolling out her dough and cutting the biscuits out with an old tin can.

"One thing I was wondering about," Johnny asked, "was why you drove all the way into town for a little dab of groceries when there is a small store just out on the highway."

Gracie quit leaning over the table and wiped her hands on an apron that was much too frilly for the blue jeans and man's western shirt she was wearing.

She used the back of her hand to push a strand of hair off her forehead. "My mother always taught me that if you can't say anything good about someone, don't say anything at all. It didn't take with me. The guy who runs that store is named Roy Wilcox. He's a crook! Plain and simple! If anything illegal or just immoral is going on around here, he's probably got his mitts in it." She shoved the sheet of biscuits in the oven and took a tub of bacon grease from the fridge. She scooped out a chunk of it and dropped it in a cast iron skillet heating on the stove.

"Like what?" Sam asked.

"Oh, he's gotten more than one family in trouble by giving them credit. After they owe him a bundle, he nicely asks that they put something up as collateral just in case they can't pay him. It's usually a car or pick-up. He gets the title. Then if they miss one payment by a few hours, he goes after their vehicle. They agree to begin with because they know they can pay when a crop comes in or they sell some livestock. Most everyone around here knows a farmer's life is controlled by crops and livestock prices. He just doesn't give a hoot!"

"Well, that's not illegal, is it?" David asked.

"No, but he's also into things no one can prove. Someone might have a bunch of pigs ready to take to market, and they get stolen the night before. Then, surprise of surprises, Roy has a load of hogs to sell at the livestock auction the next day. Everybody knows he doesn't raise pigs. Oh, he has a few to make it look good, but that's it. Pigs are kind of hard to tell one from the other. Even if they have ear tags, they can be changed."

"I can see why you'd want to stay away from him," Sam said.

Gracie was busy making gravy. "And it's not just him. All these big companies around don't care about the little guy."

Johnny noticed a tear running down her cheek. "Someone twistin' your arm, Gracie?"

She kept stirring the gravy. "Hand me some milk from the fridge, would you please?"

The milk was added, and the smells in the kitchen were getting better by the minute. She turned the heat off under the skillet and got some plates from the cabinet. Within a minute, everyone was shoveling in some great tasting food. Gracie stood by the sink, sipping her coffee.

Johnny finished his second plate and then took half a biscuit to wipe off what gravy was left. He smeared the other half with home-churned butter and fresh honey. That went down in two bites. "You never did answer my question," he said to Gracie, while still chewing the last bite of biscuit. "Who's putting the heat on you?"

"I didn't ask you boys in here to hear my problems," she said.

"Maybe we can help."

"I doubt it. Involves that old evil thing called money."

"So, someone wants money you don't have?"

She set her cup on the sink. "Anyone need another helping?"

"Not me," David said patting his stomach. "I'm full as a tick right now."

"Look," Johnny said. "You're a nice lady. Why not let us try and help you?"

"Well, that's two things I haven't been called in a long time," she said. "Nice and a lady."

"Somebody just wasn't lookin'," Johnny said. "Who wants money and how much?"

"First, the electric company. I've got two days to come up with eleven hundred dollars or they cut me off. I've been trying to pay them some, but for them, it's not enough. I guess they're gonna wait two days so they don't do it on Christmas Day and have to pay someone overtime. Big hearted souls! Then there's the propane company. They won't fill my tank right now because I haven't paid off all of last winter's bill yet. I still owe them about three hundred. I had all this worked out and someone stole the cattle I was going to sell. Guess who I think did it?"

"Good ole Roy Wilcox?" Sam said.

"Again, can't prove it. He didn't sell them around here, but I heared tell he sold some up in Monroe County right after mine disappeared. Too late by then." She took a handkerchief from her apron pocket and blew her nose. "If I lose electric, I won't be able to water any of what little stock I've got left. I've got wood stoves, but I can't get out and cut enough wood for the winter, and I sure can't afford to buy any. I'm on my last little dab right now."

Johnny pushed his chair back and stood. "Sam, David, I think I need a smoke. Let's go out on the back porch."

"You don't have to do that," Gracie said. "Willy used to smoke in here all the time."

"That's ok, ma'am. We'll go outside."

As soon as all three men were on the back porch, Sam looked at Johnny and snarled. "She can't be associated with any of that money. You're tryin' to help her, and she'll go to jail."

"Don't think so," Johnny said. "I've got an idea."

"Look," David said. "All we came back here for was to find a place to hide the money. We didn't plan on getting' mixed up with some crazy old woman."

"Just go with me on this," Johnny said.

After finishing their cigarettes, all the men returned to the kitchen. They all pitched in with the dishes. They were done and the kitchen cleaned shortly. They rounded up jugs, got them filled, and found a couple galleons of antifreeze. They loaded Gracie and the things they needed to get her on the road and took her back to where her truck was parked.

When they got there, Gracie started for the trunk. "Now, before we unload this stuff, there's something you've got to agree to do," Johnny said. "Don't agree, and we take everything and leave you here."

She stopped and wrinkled her brow at him. "What?"

Twenty minutes later, Gracie had her truck running and was headed back toward the main highway with five thousand dollars in her purse. She stopped at Wilcox's store and turned it all into money orders. Two of the money orders were for exact amounts she owed the electric company and the propane company. The rest she was supposed to get in any amounts, but keep it for herself.

Roy Wilcox thought it was very strange that this woman could come up with this much money at one time, especially when it was all in new bills, many of them with consecutive serial numbers. He kept a list behind his counter that was issued by the county sheriff for things he was to be on the look out for. He found some of the bills listed as coming from an armored car robbery in St. Louis just a couple of days ago. There was a reward listed for arrest and conviction of the person or persons involved. He was mentally spending the reward as he called the sheriff. The sheriff told him to hang on to the bills, and they would be right out after them.

The front door of his store opened as he was hanging up the phone. "Can I help you, gentlemen?"

Johnny drew a pistol from under his jacket. "Yeah, all the money you're holding in your hand. Duke, open the cash register and empty that, too."

"Just don't shoot me!" Roy begged.

"I won't, but not because you don't deserve it. I want you to go through what's coming up in your life for the next couple of days."

When the sheriff got to Wilcox's, Johnny, Sam, and David were heading north into Iowa after having stashed the rest of the robbery money under Gracie's back porch. Gracie was at her second stop and paying off the propane company. Her third stop was going to be at the bank. Her only worry was getting there before they closed early on Christmas Eve. She made it.

"So where's the money, Roy?" Sheriff Gillespie asked.

"Right after I called you, some guys came in and robbed me. They took the money."

"So who gave you the money?"

"Gracie Morgan."

"And she bought?"

"Money orders."

"So you don't have the money so we can get her prints off it?"

"No! I told you! Some guys robbed me."

"Well, Roy, I'm sorry, but there's nothing we can do." The sheriff smiled. He was well aware of many of Roy's other activities, even if he couldn't prove them.

"Get those money orders back from Gracie Morgan!" Roy shouted.

"And you can prove she used that specific money to buy those specific money orders."

Roy hung his head. "No."

"Don't know for sure, Roy, but you just might be out five grand." The sheriff started for the door. "Come to think of it, probably a little over ten

88

thousand. *If* you were really robbed of five thousand, you're still going to owe the money order people their five thousand— that is *if* you really sold the money orders. Have a nice day and Merry Christmas."

Copyright © 2008 Gary R. Hoffman

Happy Holidays Times Three

Peg Herring

Cass greeted the men who joined him at the back of the almost-empty Starbucks, raising a beefy hand to each but not raising his equally beefy frame from the seat. Despite the cold outside, Cass sipped a Coke he'd brought along with him. The kid set down something frothy and steaming; the African's drink was straight-up coffee, large and deep black, like the man himself.

Introductions were brief: "Zar, Mel. Mel, Zar." Cass revealed only enough information to prove suitability for the proposed enterprise. None of them wanted to know more than that. Mel, a twitchy, nervous kid with a sinus problem that signaled deeper concerns, was an excellent driver. He worked at a used car lot, was desperate for cash, and was not picky about how he got it. Mel fit nicely into Cass' plan.

A citizen of Kenya who'd let his green card lapse, Zar suffered from dashed delusions of grandeur. Life in America had brought no Cadillac, no easy lifestyle. Zar wanted to go home but preferred to return in style. Deportation was unacceptable. What mattered to Cass was first that Zar had worked as a security-systems installer until his recent firing and second that Zar was more afraid of the INS than the Chicago police.

Cass was all business. "I'm interested in picking up some items that can be broken up for resale. A certain person helped me find out the owners' holiday plans. My three prospects will be each away on a specific date in December."

Both men watched Cass carefully, Zar frowning as if to catch every nuance of the message, Mel eagerly, waiting for the payoff. "So which one do we hit?"

"All of them."

"What?" Mel verbalized; Zar merely waited for further explanation.

"Different holidays. Over six days we pull off three jobs where there's an empty house, a good score, and a reasonable time before the thefts are discovered."

"Let's hear what you've got." Although Mel was the vocal one, Zar's face revealed his willingness to hear more. They were in.

Cass told them some of it. His girlfriend Marilyn, who worked in a certain jewelry store, was great at chatting up the customers, making apparently idle conversation while she discovered whose homes would be empty when. It was Cass' job to figure out how to get in, how to get out, and how to get away.

* * *

When Levi Goetz brought in a brooch with a loose stone, Marilyn asked if his wife liked antique jewelry.

"No wife," Levi answered. "Just a daughter who says the thing is ugly. Still, it's an heirloom, so she'll sell it when I die. Along with everything else." He turned to go. "I leave for Florida tomorrow, but you can deliver it to my house any day but the 21st. No staff. It's the first day of Hanukkah."

* * *

"So we steal the pin on the 21st?" Mel was like a puppy you wanted to smack but really shouldn't. He couldn't help it.

"Yes. Get us a forgettable car for the night."

"I'll put plates on it from another car. If anyone remembers the number, the cops will think they got it wrong."

"Great."

"And the security system is my job." Zar's confidence pleased Cass no end, but he frowned when Zar added, "I say we stay together for the six days. No one leaves anyone else's sight." He smiled thinly. "It will keep us honest."

Cass considered. "Fine. We can stay at my place. Now, I'll deal with the safe, which ain't much. Goetz is a good starting point, an easy score."

And it was. The job went off without a hitch. Mel stood watch at from a spot down the street in case someone took an interest in the Goetz place. Zar handled the rather antiquated alarm efficiently. They entered the musty old house, bypassing a beautiful old Menorah too big to cart away.

Cass took apart the ancient safe in no time at all, spilling the brooch from its velvet pouch into his hand with a gleeful grin. "Step one, complete!"

But it wasn't quite that easy. They left the house,

separating and circling around to the next block as tiny, stinging flakes of snow hit their faces. Zar carried a gym bag slung over his shoulder like a guy headed to his athletic club for a workout. Inside it were their burglars' tools and the jewel-studded brooch.

As they reached the car, Zar's restless eyes revealed his nervousness. Mel was a wreck, but he was also ecstatic. "Did you get it? Was it really that easy? Can I see?"

"Calm down," Cass ordered, but he had to smile at the kid's enthusiasm. "Let's get out of here in case some little old lady is staring out the window instead of lighting her Hanukkah candles."

Mel hit the remote as Zar moved to the passenger side. They all froze at the same moment. Across the back seat lay a body, a woman who might have been sleeping except for the large knife sticking out of her chest.

"What the—?"

"Shut up," Cass ordered. "Get in the car."

"But she's—"

"Shut up. We've got to move fast."

They got it. They were holding a stolen brooch. There was a dead woman in their car. They needed time to deal with this disaster. Gulping back their reluctance, the men opened the doors and got in, Mel driving, Zar in the front. Cass clambered into the back, actually sitting on the corpse's feet. In seconds they were safely away.

They dumped the body under the El tracks late

that night, in a spot where it would not be found soon. People avoided the area, at least the sort of people who might actually report a dead body. Cass did the heavy work while the other two stood lookout. As he came back to the car Mel asked, "Who do you think she is?"

"No idea."

"Who put her in our car?"

"Couldn't say."

"How did they get her in it? It was locked."

Finally Cass growled, "Kid, I don't know. Zar doesn't know. We got handed a load of crap, and we got rid of it. Now concentrate on the next job."

"We're gonna go on?"

"Why not? This had nothing to do with us. Somebody needed to get rid of a body, and they chose our car."

Mel looked doubtful, but Zar added, "I for one do not want to give up future revenue because of an unlucky circumstance."

So just as December 25, arrived, bringing the pretty, fluffy snow every Christmas should have, the three approached the house where Michael J. Smith would be found had he been at home. Every home on the block was decorated for Christmas, some minimally and some with the manic conspicuous consumption that only Americans achieve.

* * *

When Smith brought in a stunning diamond necklace for insurance evaluation Marilyn asked, "A gift for your wife?"

Smith's grin was rueful. "A peace offering due to a small indiscretion." The way he regarded Marilyn's chest hinted that Mr. Smith had not learned a lesson. Instead he'd decided it was worth it to play and then pay up. "We're going to ski Vail and come back late Christmas day. The box will be under the tree. She'll be totally surprised."

***

And so would he, Cass thought with a chuckle. Anyone so dumb as to leave a prize like that out in the open deserved to get it stolen. Especially after bragging about it to a clerk whose boyfriend happened to be a jewel thief.

Smith had no live-in servants, so the house was empty. The problem was that the guy's alarm was pretty good. Cass was glad for Zar's expertise, because he couldn't have bypassed this particular system. Ironically, there was a damn good safe in the house, but Smith's desire to have his wife find the necklace under the tree had overcome common sense. He approached the massive fir on hands and knees lest some passer-by see someone in the Smith house. It was decorated in peach and white, which disgusted Cass. "Christmas colors are red and green. People should stick with that."

Outside the two performed their dance of separation and reunion again, reaching another "borrowed" car several blocks away as Mel crossed the street to join them.

At the car Mel gasped, Zar groaned, and Cass

muttered, "I don't believe it."

This time there was no knife, but the white face and the chest wound confirmed death. And to make things worse... "It's the same girl," Mel said in a strangled voice.

It was the body they'd disposed of four days ago. Cass reached out and touched the ankle that extended toward him. "She's really cold."

"No surprise. It's freezing out here."

"Someone brought her back to us."

"Why?"

"I don't know."

"What do we do now?"

Cass seemed to shake off his confusion. "We go. We get rid of the body again. Then we figure this out."

This time they drove into Wisconsin, Mel assuring that no one followed. They found an unattended rest area and Cass carried the body, wrapped in a blanket, far into the woods behind it. The others hollowed out a place in the deep snow and he laid the dead woman face down in it. They kicked snow over her until she was no longer visible. "Good till spring, probably," Cass said by way of graveside service.

It was noon on Christmas Day before they returned to town. "Good thing the dealership's closed," Mel muttered. They dropped off the car, walked to where Cass' Pontiac sat, and got in. Zar took the necklace out of the box and laid it across his lap, a visible reward for an unsettling night's work.

"So do we quit now?" Mel sounded hopeful.

"I vote no."

"But somebody's out to get us."

"But they didn't. And now that we know it, we'll be more careful."

"They know where we're going to be. They get into the car. They found where we put the body."

"So they followed us. They have some way of unlocking the car."

Mel frowned. "Maybe the tennis ball thing."

"What?"

"You drill a hole in a tennis ball and then push it up against the lock. The air pressure opens the door."

"Whatever." Cass was impatient. "We'll just be sure they don't succeed again."

"So we do the third job?"

"Yes." Cass' gaze moved to Zar, who straightened as if throwing a weight off the back of his neck.

"I agree. But we keep careful watch every step of the way."

"But it's tomorrow, and we haven't slept. Ain't you tired?"

Cass grinned with a glint of his old confidence. "When we're rich we can sleep all we want."

December 26th dawned cold and clear. Mel was almost manic. "I should stay by the van. Maybe they won't—"

"We hid her good, and we need you inside to help find the safe. Now relax."

Mel started their latest "loaner" and accelerated smoothly onto the road. They were dressed as repairmen, and their van had a magnetic logo strip that read "Werman Plumbing." Each man had a toolbox and a hat with the same logo. They had practiced the businesslike, head-down walk of the repairman on the job. Cass even had a clipboard with a phony repair order. If anyone asked, they were ready.

Martin Chisolm, prominent African-American attorney with an eye to future political office, had recently purchased a jeweled Nemji doll. Unlike most Nemjis, this one sported real gems that were worth plenty. Chisolm had brought it to the shop to be mounted on a base so he could present it to the African-American Center during Kwanzaa.

* * *

"I'm not sure I understand Kwanzaa." Marilyn batted her eyes at Chisolm.

There followed a lengthy description of its origins, observances, and benefits for the community. In the process Marilyn learned that Chisolm would host the festivities at Fosco Park on the first day of Kwanzaa. His family would attend with him. The presentation of the doll was slated for the third day of Kwanzaa, December 28th.

"If you leave the box behind," Marilyn told Cass later, "he won't realize it's gone for a day, maybe two."

* * *

Puffing cloudy breaths into the frigid air, the men made a show of ringing Chisolm's doorbell and waiting. Zar walked around the house as if looking for signs of life. An expert maneuver disabled the alarm, and he returned to the front with an exaggerated shrug to indicate frustration. As Cass turned as if to ring the bell again, Mel blocked the view while he popped the lock. The door swung open, and they pretended to speak with someone inside the house. Cass indicated the truck, showed his clip board, and nodded several times. Finally they went inside and closed the door.

On a table in the foyer Kwanzaa gifts were scattered around a centerpiece: the fruit, grain, and cup laid out on a mat along with seven candles. Under it all lay a brightly-colored cloth of black, red, and green. Cass had hoped the doll might be on display, but it was not.

They'd been unable to ascertain ahead of time where the safe was located. Plumbing repairs, however, are notoriously time-intensive. They split up, spent half an hour searching likely places, and were finally rewarded when Mel called, "It's in here."

Cass went to work. "Not the worst I've tackled," he muttered, kneeling over the spot in the floor where the safe was situated. "Maybe a half hour."

It was more like forty-five minutes, but the doll was worth it. Its leather coat was studded with rubies, its eyes were diamonds, and what looked like gold wire wrapped its arms, legs, neck, and middle.

They put the doll in a toolbox, cleaned the place of anything that might identify them, and left. The van sat at the curb, and, recalling earlier experiences, they approached with caution. Mel peered into the front seat and sighed with relief that was, sadly, premature. When they opened the back to stow their new-found wealth, there was the body, now slack, smelly, and much the worse for wear. Mel retched, and Zar's dark face turned slightly gray at the sight.

"Damn," Cass whispered hoarsely.

The smell from the van was disturbing, but something held Zar's attention. "There's a note."

Cass leaned in, gingerly took the single sheet of paper from off the corpse's chest then shut the van doors to hide their macabre cargo. Four words gave a single, unequivocal command. "Give it all back."

"Who are these guys? What do they want?"

"They want us put back what we've taken." Zar sounded resigned.

"But why? How?"

Mel's questions were really starting to wear on Cass. "I don't know."

Zar looked around nervously. "Someone knows where we'll be and what we're doing. They know where we dumped the body. Twice. They know a lot about us."

"But wh—"

"We DON'T KNOW, kid. Get it? We DON'T KNOW!"

"It's your contact at the jewelry store. You said she knows about the jobs," Mel said, his voice heavy.

"It ain't Marilyn."

"It has to be. Maybe you don't know her as well as you think."

"That's her." Cass' voice was almost a whisper.

"What?"

"It's her in there. I didn't want to scare you. I needed the money, but now..."

There was a shocked silence. Mel's eyes kept sweeping the area. "I say we do it."

"Do what?"

"Give the stuff back."

"No!" Realizing their argument was public, Cass forced himself to control his reaction. "No. We got the stuff. It's ours now."

Zar looked from one to the other, thinking it over. "I agree with Mel. It isn't worth it. If they killed your girlfriend, they'll kill us, too."

"But it doesn't make sense."

"No, it doesn't, but they could call the cops even if they don't kill us. Who says we didn't stab Marilyn?"

"So we go back to return the stuff and the cops are there waiting for us?"

A pause, then Cass said, "I suppose we could mail it."

"Mail it?"

"Yeah, make up three parcels, drop them at a post office, and get clear." His jaw went tight. "But no. There has to be a way to keep what we've got."

Neither Mel nor Zar wanted any part of the scheme now that a dead body was linked to them and its purpose made clear. Cass offered to take the responsibility, fence the goods, and deliver their cuts to them, but they refused, possibly due to the corpse in

Happy Holidays Times Three

the van or possibly from general mistrust. In the end Zar returned to the post office idea. Mel agreed, effectively out-voting Cass. They made a quick plan. Cass went along, still muttering about diamonds and living on the Mexican Riviera.

"It's over, Cass," Zar said firmly. "This is something we didn't anticipate. Let's get out of it while we can."

Redemption began with stopping at a dollar store where they picked up three generic mailers. Wearing surgical gloves, Zar placed the brooch in one, the necklace in another, and the doll in a third, larger one. He wrapped them securely with brown mailing tape. Then they visited the public library, where they printed off the addresses of their three victims. Once again wearing gloves, Zar cut labels and taped one on the front of each box.

Once the parcels were ready, they stopped off at a Goodwill store and then drove to three different post offices. Cass mailed the packages, one at each stop, wearing a different baseball cap and nondescript sweatshirt each time. Zar and Mel watched through the glass. No one paid him any particular attention at all.

"It should be okay," Cass said when they'd finished. "How hard are the cops gonna look for thieves who returned what they took anyway?"

"What about Marilyn?"

Cass stared at the rear section of the van with obvious repugnance. "Head for my place, but make sure we aren't followed."

Mel was good. He ducked and dived through traffic, never breaking a law or drawing notice. They were sure when they arrived at Cass' building that no one was behind them. "If they know what we're doing, they know where you live," Zar said.

"I thought of that. We won't be here for long." Cass' apartment was on the ground floor, accessed almost directly from the parking lot. His beat-up Grand Am sat in front of 3A, and Mel parked the van next to it. Leading the way to the back of the building to a row of storage units for the apartment dwellers, Cass opened one with a small silver key. "We're gonna need a few things from here."

He ducked inside the crowded space and came out with an old sleeping bag. "I'll put Marilyn in this. You guys find some rope and the spud that's here somewhere."

"What's a spud?"

Cass rolled his eyes and sighed. "The handle looks like a shovel but the blade is a lot smaller. It chops through ice."

When Mel and Zar arrived with the two requested items, Cass was just zipping the sleeping bag closed. Mel seemed relieved that the corpse was no longer visible. "We drop her into a lake with some weight attached," Cass announced. "I'd like to see somebody bring her back from that." As he wiped his hands on the outside of the bag, the others looked away. He was one cold customer.

Mel removed the insignia so that the former

plumber's conveyance was simply an unremarkable green van. They started off well past midnight toward a lake Cass said was fairly deserted this time of year. "I ice fish, know all the good spots."

Still watchful for tailing vehicles, they moved through the suburbs and into a less inhabited area. From the back of the van Cass directed Mel with curt commands, apparently unconcerned about sharing space with his dead girlfriend. The smell alone was enough to make the other two sick, and for once Mel had no questions.

At the lake, they piled out of the van into a wind so cold it burned. Cass pulled the sleeping bag from the back and hefted it onto his shoulder. Mel got the spud, the rope and a flashlight. Zar rolled the van's spare tire along beside them to provide the weight. As the three trudged out onto the frozen lake, Mel's question gene kicked back in. "How do you know the ice will hold us?"

"It's a foot deep. That's good enough."

"So we gotta dig through a foot of ice?"

"Yeah."

"Why can't we just bury her somewhere?"

"This is easier. The ice fills in the hole, the wind blows away our tracks, and no one can tell we were here. If she's ever found, the water will have ruined any evidence."

"Oh."

They took turns chopping at the ice. Mel's clumsy effort eventually hit slush. After that they worked to widen the hole sufficiently for their purpose.

With the heavy tire punctured to release the air and tied to it, the sleeping bag with its grisly contents disappeared into the hole with hardly a sound. Mel watched it go and said in an attempt at sympathy, "Sorry about your girlfriend, Cass."

"Yeah." There wasn't much emotion to it. Maybe Cass and Marilyn hadn't been that close.

The three separated when they got back to the city. Mel would return the van to the car lot and put in his normal day's work, despite recent dreams of wealth and Vegas. He said a diffident farewell and drove away. Zar simply faded into the night, on foot and no closer to Africa than when they began.

Cass returned to his apartment, letting himself in with a sense of relief. It was a long time since he'd been warm, a long week of stress and worry. It was all worth it when Marilyn greeted him with an enthusiastic kiss.

"Everything go all right, baby?"

"Fine. Your kitty-litter-filled look-alike is at the bottom of Lake Cronus."

"I don't look much like an inflatable doll, but good for her. I was tired of playing dead."

Cass grinned. "But you did it so well. The makeup job got better each time. And getting the dummy into the van before they came along with the spud took some doing."

Marilyn smiled at the praise. "The worst part was the cold, and then getting the limburger smell out of my hair. But you played them real good, sweetie."

Cass was not particularly modest. "I gotta admit it was fun letting them convince me what to do next."

"They went for the post office idea?"

"Like shoppers at a holiday sale. I mailed the packets to myself, put a stick-on label over the original before I slid the package over to the postal clerk."

Marilyn shivered. "I thought for sure one of them would touch me to see if I was really dead."

"Who wants to touch a corpse? They were glad to let me handle it—I mean, you."

Marilyn grinned. "So it worked. Three scores and no divvying at all."

Cass opened a beer. "Happy Hanukkah, Merry Christmas, and Kwanzaa Peace, baby. Now we wait for the mailman to bring us really happy holidays."

Copyright © 2008 Peg Herring

Taking Her Medicine

Tony Burton

Maureen O'Malley would never walk again in her life. Or bowl in the church league for Saint Monica's. Or even tie her own shoes. All those, and a thousand other more mundane things, were taken away from her by 3,600 pounds of hurtling steel, glass and plastic. And the driver of the car that struck her was drunk… plastered… three sheets to the wind.

People give bland, innocuous names to the things that embarrass them, but they don't have the guts or the desire to stop. Adultery is "stepping out." Cheating on an exam is "cribbing." Using cocaine is "getting high."

Jessica Stone was sorry it happened. Very sorry. But not sorry enough to stop drinking and driving, because she ended up six months later with a broken wrist caused by another drunk driving accident. And at this moment she was sitting in Beaudry's Sports Bar, nursing a scotch and soda. It wasn't her usual hangout, but The Crow Bar was too quiet tonight.

"Seriously, I can't believe they wanted to take my license permanently!" she said to the bartender, who only shook his head as he polished a glass. "I've only had one other DUI, where I hit that woman back in May… well, there was that other one down in Ohio, but they don't know about that one here," she mumbled. She gulped the rest of her drink as the bar stereo encouraged everyone there to have a holly, jolly

Christmas.

A well-dressed young man with reddish-blonde hair sat down beside her. "Diet Coke," he said, and the bartender nodded and filled a glass from a multi-buttoned dispenser hose. Jessica eyed the young man. *Not bad looking, and well-dressed, too.*

She sighed dramatically, and he looked over at her. As the bartender sat his drink on a bar coaster in front of him, the young man said, "Problem? That sounded pretty serious." He nodded to her and sipped his drink. "My name's Terry," he said by way of introduction. "Yours?"

"Jessica, and it's sorta serious, yeah." She pointed to the cast on her wrist. "I was in a car accident a few days ago, and this hurts sometimes. But the real bummer is that they suspended my license because I was drinking when it happened." She swirled the ice in her now-empty glass. "Makes it difficult for a girl, you know?"

Terry nodded. "Yeah, it would put a cramp in anyone's lifestyle. Anyone else injured in the accident?"

Jessica considered for a moment and lied by shaking her head. The little boy would be out of the hospital in a few weeks, anyway. She swirled her ice again, with a painful grimace at her wrist.

"Don't you take anything for the pain?"

"Yeah, Havadol, but I'm not s'posed to take it when I'm drinking." She fished a small pillbox from her purse and showed him the tiny tablets inside it, closed it and dropped it on the counter. Brian picked up the box and looked at the enameled lid. "They said it would be dangerous to mix it with alcohol, so I always wait till I'm home and settled down before I take any." She smiled a little. "The scotch helps a little," she said, with a hopeful glance at the bartender's back.

Terry got the bartender's attention and had him refill Jessica's highball glass, this time with Dewar's and no soda. "There, that should dull the pain even more," he said with a smile.

"Ooh, thanks, Terry. Real sweet of you!" She took a swallow of the scotch, and looked him over with an appraising eye. She noticed the lack of a wedding ring. "I need to go to the little girl's room, and it's almost time for me to head home. You doing anything later?"

Terry looked down into his glass. "Well, I had plans, but…."

Jessica, emboldened by his pause, laid her hand on his thigh and squeezed a little. "You think you could change them, for me?" The liquor had really loosened her up, and she leaned in closer. "It's not that far to my place," she whispered, her breath caressing his ear.

She saw Terry flush, and smiled to herself. She stood up. "I'll be right back, and then you can walk me home. It's dark out, and I don't like walking in the cold by myself."

He stood up then. "Never let it be said that I'm not a gentleman." He paid their tab, and she wove her way to the restroom. In a few minutes she was back, and swallowed the rest of the scotch in her glass.

They made their way to the door, Jessica stumbling a little and bumping against him. "Oopsie! Sorry, Terry..." but he waved it off.

"Don't worry about it. Here, take my arm." He opened the door, and the bell jingled over their heads.

She smiled as she took the offered arm, and leaned in tightly, pressing her thigh against his. "Thanks. Makes it easier."

He gave her a strangely crooked smile. "Yeah, it does make it easier."

They proceeded down Fourteenth for a couple of blocks, over the river, past Jefferson Avenue and Franklin. The colorful lights and fake candy canes on the lamp posts were festive, but the spitting snow blowing in the cold wind took their mind away from enjoying the sight. They stopped at the Henderson Building and Terry reached for the door, but it was locked and there was no one behind the doorman's desk. He looked at Jessica.

"Don' worry, Terry. Got a key from the doorman about a year ago. Cost me two bottles of bourbon, but it's handy when he's on a potty break." She fumbled with trying to get the key into the lock, so Terry took it from her and unlocked the door, ushering her in. She didn't mention what else the key had cost her, but figured that wasn't any of Terry's business, anyway.

The elevator ride up was quick and quiet. Fourth floor, turn right, second door on the right.

Jessica's apartment was shabby chic, with a little elf-high Christmas tree sitting on a table by the window. She kicked off her shoes and dropped her purse as she entered. "Relax, Terry… take off your coat and visit for a while." She disappeared into the back of the apartment. "Make me a drink, will you?" she called from out of sight.

Terry looked around for the bar, and found a couple of bottles sitting on a table near the stereo. He fixed up a drink for her and handed it to her wrapped in a napkin as she walked into the room. Jessica now wore a dark red silk robe that reached the tops of her knees. "Mmmm… just what I need," she said as she looked at him and took a large sip. "C'mere an' sit with me on the sofa," she said as she tugged at his sleeve. "An' you're still wearin' your coat, silly man!"

Jessica collapsed onto the sofa, showing a long expanse of tanned thigh, and he sat down more carefully beside her, still wearing his coat. Terry pointed at her plaster-wrapped wrist. "I thought you took your medicine after you got home, so your wrist won't hurt."

She looked at the cast on her wrist, blinking like it surprised her to find it there. "Oh. Yeah, now I'm home, guess I can take it. Won't matter if I pass out now." She giggled. "You wouldn't take advantage of a girl, would you?" She batted her eyes at him and he smiled that crooked smile again.

"Not a chance," he replied as he got up and walked across the room to pick up her purse, returning to place it in her lap. "You just need to take your medicine, and worry about me some other time."

She fumbled around in her purse, having difficulty with finding her pillbox. "Here, let me get it for you," Terry said, retrieving the pillbox and opening it for her. She scraped a tablet out and held it in her hand. "Man, I gotta refill that thing. I thought there was more left in there than that!"

"Do you want some water?"

She eyed him, then downed the pills with the rest of her drink. "Who needs water when I have this nice drink you made me." She leered at him. "Hey, let's have some Christmas music," she said and eased to her feet after a couple of giggling attempts. She stumbled to the stereo and punched a button. The mellow sounds of Bing Crosby crooning "White Christmas" issued from the speakers and she turned around with a smile.

Jessica moved her feet in a little dance step, but as she approached the sofa she stopped, blinking. "Wha... what's the matter wi' me?" The empty glass slipped from her hand, bouncing on the old berber carpet. "I feel... funny... woozy." She took two steps and collapsed toward Terry. He caught her without saying a word, and eased her onto the sofa cushions.

Terry stood, looking down at her for a moment, then moved to the other end of the sofa and gently lifted her feet, placing them so she lay fully on the cushions. He put one of the throw pillows under her head, arranging her hair carefully around her face. "Terry... wha... matter wi' me?" she repeated, her voice slurring the words and her unfocused eyes blinking up at him.

Terry knelt on the floor beside the sofa. "Jessica, I'm sorry to have to do this. But you can't continue this way." He leaned down and softly kissed her brow, which furrowed as he did. Her lips moved, but she didn't say anything.

"At least this is easier than what I originally planned. Wouldn't you rather die here in your own warm, cozy apartment, than drown in that cold, icy river, half-drunk?" Her eyes opened wider, but she still didn't say anything. He nodded. "Oh, yes. The plan was to get you nice and drunk, then give you a shove into the river as we walked across the bridge… or maybe as we went for a romantic stroll beside it."

She tried to speak, but her voice was a mumbled gargling sound, and her eyelids kept dropping shut.

Terry continued as he stroked her hair, "But you made it easy. Showing me your medicine, bringing me back here and asking me to fix your drink while you got ready to seduce me. I'm gay, did you know that?" He laughed a bitter laugh. "But you don't know me, do you? It doesn't matter, anyway."

He shook her and she dragged her eyes open. "Hey, wake up! I want you to know what happened. I put one of your pain pills in your drink at the bar, two in the drink you just finished off and you just took one more along with them."

Her lips moved as though she tried to speak, but no sound came from her.

"Why?" He stood up, picked up her glass from the floor and took it to the kitchen to rinse it, then splashed a little more liquor in it before setting it on the coffee table. "I guess you could call it revenge, but I think it's a higher, more sacred thing than that."

Her eyes closed again, and her breathing grew so shallow as to be almost undetectable. Terry took the other throw pillow from the sofa and pressed it tightly on her face. In less than a minute, even the slight movement of her chest stopped, and he tucked the pillow alongside the other one under her head, once more arranging her hair. With his handkerchief he wiped off anything he had touched: the glass, the keys, the pillbox, her purse, the liquor bottles, the faucet handles in the sink. He took her now-flaccid hand and touched her fingers to the pillbox, and wrapped them around the highball glass and scotch bottle.

Bing had moved on to "Silent Night" before Terry let himself out and went down the elevator to the parking garage. He walked out past the electronic gate, and the four blocks to his car. He was cold inside and out, but there was no regret.

As he let himself into his house, he heard the sound of his mother's power wheelchair moving through the house. Her wheezy voice asked, "Brian? Is that you?"

"Yes, mom, it's me." He hung his coat on a peg in the hallway, then went to greet her with a kiss on the cheek. "You doing OK?"

She smiled at him. "I'm fine. Good to see you

made it home safe, Brian. You know what the crazies are like out there nowadays!" She backed and turned her wheelchair expertly, using slight motions of her head to control the mechanism. Six months of use had made its operation easier.

"It's OK, Mom. Mrs. O'Malley didn't raise any stupid children, you know?" He walked into their kitchen. "You want some eggnog?"

Copyright ©2007, Tony Burton

A Christmas Carole

Janice Alonso

Marley was dead, to begin with. There was no doubt whatever about that. Carole Mitchell looked down at her elderly neighbor Marley Jones, his expression rigid from the overnight freezing temperatures, his lower body collecting the newest layer of late-December snow.

And Marley had been murdered, to end with. There was no doubt whatever about that either. The blow had been to the back of the head, and the blood had flowed through his knit cap and iced into red fingers that clung to his face and neck. A terra cotta flower pot lay shattered beside him, summer dirt still stuck to the jagged shards.

Sheriff Jorge Vasquez crouched closer and studied the remains of his friend. Marley twisted at an awkward angle, his upper body protected beneath the porch while his lower half protruded outward into the elements. Vasquez straightened, his knees popping. "I'm sorry you had to be the one to find him, Cici."

Carole had been nicknamed Christmas Carole, shortened to Cici, because she whittled and hand-painted Christmas ornaments.

Her eyes brimmed. "Such a dear, sweet man. Why would anyone want to hurt him?"

"A bigger question is *why* would he have ventured out on the coldest night of the year?"

Vasquez removed a handkerchief from his back pocket and extended it toward Cici. "You said you left his house at eight last night?"

She nodded and took the handkerchief, blotting away her tears. "I cooked Marley a couple of meals so he wouldn't have to worry about food in case he got snowed in." Her voice grew softer. "I tried to get him to come home with me, but he refused. Didn't want to leave Butler." A weak smile broke through as she thought about the handsome Maine Coon mix, named after the dashing Rhett Butler. The cat was Marley's best friend in the world, and he was probably Butler's only friend. Cici had never known a meaner, more cantankerous creature in her life. Now what would become of him? He wouldn't let anyone except Marley come within ten feet without a showdown. Marley had rescued him a few years back on a morning after a night as cold as last night. Butler had been weeks old and more than half dead when Marley had heard the kitten mewling under his back porch. Since then Butler had grown into 30-plus pounds of pure muscle, running through Marley's cabin knocking everything in his path into disarray.

"I'm sure Jennifer can handle him." A smile played at the corners of Vasquez's lips. "I swear the woman was raised by a pack of wildcats herself." Jennifer Smith was the area veterinarian by trade, but she was also a poet with a gentle heart and had tamed the wildest of animals in her career.

Cici's smile broadened as she agreed with Vazquez's assessment. "Do you want me to ask her?"

She paused, realization of the situation settling in. "*Oh!* She doesn't even know about Marley's death yet, does she?"

The sheriff looked at his watch. "Why don't you come back in about an hour? The medical examiner and the Criminal Investigation Division should be here by then." He ran a hand across his unshaven chin. "We can't touch this area 'til they get here."

She nodded and left Vasquez to wait for the forensic team. Ice draped the tall firs and bowed their branches. Trudging her way through the snow, Cici listened to the ice tinkling as it broke free of the trees and shattered to the ground. The morning sun glinted off the frozen lake and sparkled with a freshness that she could not absorb. All was quiet save for the whistle of a distant wind and the crunch of her boots on the trail.

When she came to Jennifer's cabin, Cici mounted the stairs and lifted the heavy knocker, banging it several times. An evergreen wreathe with red velvet bows and bright holly berries hung on the door.

The curtain on the side window fluttered. Jennifer looked out and saw her neighbor's pinched expression, then rushed to the door.

"What's wrong?" Jennifer's mop of chestnut-colored curls separated into clumps where she'd not brushed out the morning bed-head. Opening the door wider, she motioned for Cici to come in.

Cici wrapped her arms around Jennifer, patting her back as she related the news of poor Marley's demise.

"When did you find him?" asked Jennifer.

"About eight-thirty when I started out for my walk... I stopped by his house to see if he wanted anything from town. I called Jorge and he rushed over."

Jennifer ran her fingers through her hair. "Give me a few minutes to get cleaned up and we'll get Butler."

* * *

By ten-thirty Jennifer and Cici stood with Vasquez, two EMTs, and three crime scene specialists.

"We've got Butler locked in the laundry room," said Vasquez. "His crate's in the garage."

Cici faced Vasquez as Jennifer left with the examiner to get the cat. "Have you been inside?" she asked.

He nodded. "Everything seemed normal." A gust of wind rose and blew a dusting of snow into his face. "I went through each room. His dinner plates had been washed and placed on the counter, and he'd cut a piece of your chocolate cake—"

"Chocolate cake?" Cici's face scrunched in confusion. "I didn't bring dessert... didn't see it when I was there either."

"The slice of cake was sitting on his desk. I assumed you brought it." Vasquez added the new information to his notes. "He even had a fork lying next to the plate and a mug filled with coffee."

"But something interrupted him?" asked Cici.

"Could have been someone at the door, or maybe he heard a noise." He shrugged. "Once the CID is through, we'll have a better idea of what might have happened."

"How awful," Cici said.

"The rest of the room points to some sort of interruption. The logs were ready in the fireplace but not lit, and he had a student's paper spread across the desk—like he was ready to settle in for the evening."

Cici's face paled. "Jorge, Marley canceled his writing class yesterday. He told me he was going to read a western he bought at the book store earlier in the week, and..." Her voice began to shake, "Marley said the only thing missing would be a fire because he hadn't any wood."

"We're ready," Jennifer called, lugging the crate with Butler, an arch-backed mess of hisses, matted fur, and exposed claws. She held up an arm wrapped in a bandage. "He put up a great battle, but I won." She glanced at a stream of blood oozing from the covering. "I think. By the way, I couldn't find his litter box."

"He doesn't have one. Marley installed a little door for him in the kitchen," explained Cici.

She returned her attention to Vasquez, "Then, I wasn't the only one there."

Vasquez's eyes narrowed. "Dinner, chocolate cake, firewood, and a paper." He held up his fingers. "Marley may have had *four* visitors last night."

* * *

Later that afternoon Cici sat in the largest room at the Lawtonville Arts Center facing rows of folding chairs set up for the monthly Saturday meeting. Lawtonville, a small town tucked south of the Georgia/Tennessee line, had become a haven for artists over the years. With a back drop of the Appalachian Mountains mirrored in Lake Chattooga, the town provided a bottomless well of inspiration. Marley Jones, a retired professor of creative writing, had been the founder of the Lawtonville Arts Guild. As President of the Guild, the duty of telling the members about Marley fell to Cici.

She watched as people trickled inside from the frigid outdoors. Mac and Julie Goldberg sat on the front row and sipped their oversized lattes from Herman's Coffee Den. Mac and Julie were the co-authors of the popular Stedman Garth Mystery series. Next to them sat Bud Dermott, covered in dust from head to toe and the only sculptor in the guild. He chatted with Lindsay Peterman, an actress/writer. Jennifer sat up front with Cici.

"We'll start when Jorge arrives," Cici said.

At three o'clock on the dot, Sheriff Vasquez walked through the door, stomped the snow from his shoes, and removed his hat.

Cici stood. "Before we get started with our meeting, I'm afraid we have some terrible news." Her voice broke as she related the morbid details once again. "Jorge will tell us what he's found out and answer questions."

Vasquez cleared his throat and walked to the front of the room. "It appears Marley died around midnight last night. He was hit with a flower pot that sat on the railing of his back porch." He paused before adding, "We think the pot's impact knocked him unconscious and then during the night, Marley froze to death. The county lab has his body."

"And you're *sure* it was murder," gasped Mac. "Here in Lawtonville?"

"I'm afraid so... unless Marley conked himself over the back of the head with the flower pot." Vasquez shoved his hands into his pockets. "There was blood on the pot that I'm sure will match Marley's."

"Do you have any suspects?" asked Lindsay.

"No, but that brings me to an uncomfortable subject." Vasquez shifted his weight to his other foot, his face shading pink. "I'm going to need to question each of you as to your whereabouts and relationship with Marley."

Bud Dermott stood. "Surely you don't believe any of us did poor Marley in!" His tone moved from one of anger to one of sorrow. "We all loved Marley. He was everybody's friend." Tears streamed into his grizzly beard. "That man stayed by my side during the dreadful ordeal with Lucia." Bud's wife Lucia had died with liver cancer the past spring.

"And when we were trying to get our Stedman Garth series off the ground, Marley referred us to the best agent in New York." Julie blew her nose into a tissue and nodded. "It had to be some sort of vagrant or a—"

"There are no *vagrants* around here, Julie," spat

Bud. "Lawtonville is fifty miles from nowhere. And as steep as that mountain road is and all the snow we got last night, if someone did wander in, he sure could have never wandered out." He brought up two clenched fists. "If *I'm* the one who finds this person, I'll kill him myself... with my bare hands!"

"Calm down." Vasquez held up his hands. "Getting angry isn't helping the situation." His voice held steady. "Now I know Cici was there. Anyone else happen to visit Marley last night?"

Bud spoke again. "I took him some firewood in case we lost power."

Lindsay raised her hand. "And I took over my screenplay since he canceled the writing class yesterday." Fresh tears flowed. "But I didn't notice anything suspicious."

Vasquez waited, then asked, "Anyone take him a chocolate cake?"

"I did," came a weak voice from Julie.

Vasquez added the names to his notes. He looked up. "I'll begin the interrogations with you four tomorrow... I'll get to the rest of you later." His slipped the pad into his jacket pocket.

All eyes followed Vasquez as he strode to the back of the room and out the door, but no one said a word.

Cici found her voice first. "So, what Jorge means is..." Her eyes met Jennifer's, "he thinks one of us is the murderer."

* * *

The following morning Jennifer and Cici sat

across from each other at a little table in the front window at Herman's. Outside Christmas lights twinkled on the tree set up in the main square, and across the street a manger scene stood on the front lawn of the First Baptist Church.

"One of us?" Jennifer repeated the words. "This is surreal."

"And with most of the residents out of town for the holidays, it comes down to a few of us." Cici leaned in closer and whispered. "A *very few* of us."

"This is beginning to sound like an Agatha Christie cozy." Jennifer wrapped her hands around her cup of steaming green tea.

"I can't even think about it," said Cici. As she lifted the cappuccino to her lips, the door to the coffee shop opened.

Deputy John Tym, Vasquez's assistant, entered and walked over to them.

"Jorge is ready for you," he said.

Cici and Jennifer followed Deputy Tym across the square to the Lawtonville Courthouse and sat in the waiting room.

"Morning," said the woman sitting at the desk in the reception area. Her hair was worked into tight cornrows, little streaks of gray winding their way through each braid. From her lobes dangled tiny candy cane earrings.

"Hi, Tameka," said Cici.

"I can't believe Marley's dead," she said. Her lips were swathed with a rich mocha-colored lipstick, and the corners of her mouth pulled downward. "Just last week he was helping me decide on the music my dance class will perform for Kwanzaa this year." Her large brown eyes filled with tears.

"His death leaves such an empty space in this town, but at least he's left a legacy with the Arts Guild." Jennifer folded Tameka's hands into hers. "We missed you at the meeting on Saturday."

"Yeah, I don't think you've ever missed a meeting," said Cici. "Is everything okay?"

"I wasn't feeling well... up all night with a headache... spent most of the day in bed." Tameka's voice quavered. "I didn't even know about Marley until last night."

Lindsay and Vasquez emerged from his private office. Lindsay's eyes were red-rimmed and her face splotched.

"Jennifer, I'll take you next," said Vasquez.

"I need to go to the storeroom," said Tameka.

After Jennifer and Vasquez disappeared behind the closed door, Cici turned to Lindsay. "What did Jorge ask?"

"It was just horrible. Explaining my whereabouts on Friday night wasn't so bad. I was home watching a movie." Her shoulders slumped. "But I don't have anyone to vouch for me."

"Well, *who* will?" comforted Cici. "It was such bad weather I'd think everyone was home." She shook her head. "And since only a few of us live with anyone, hardly anybody will have someone to alibi for what we were doing."

"I gave a timeline of my visit with Marley . . . what I saw and said... what I *didn't* see or say. I had to recreate *every* conversation I've had with Marley this past week and fill out pages and pages of information about my background." She twisted the tissue in her hand. "I'm so upset I don't know if half of what I said was accurate or not."

"We're all in the same boat," reassured Cici.

"The worst part was explaining about our writing class and why I took my paper over when the class had been canceled." Her face flamed. "I was just so excited about my latest draft I couldn't wait until next week." She buried her face in her hands. "Now I'm a murder suspect!"

Cici placed a hand on Lindsay's shoulder. "Who else is in the workshop?"

"There are five of us. I'm the only one who lives in Lawtonville," she sniffed. "The rest are from Cleveland."

"In Tennessee?" asked Cici.

"Yes, but it's only a forty-five minute drive. They come as a group for the class each week," said Lindsay.

Cici's eyebrows arched. "Did anyone in the class have something against Marley?"

Lindsay shook her head no. "Not that I know of." She sighed. "I told Jorge everything I know about them." Pursing her lips, she continued. "Jorge already has the class roster and sent one of his men to talk to them."

The outside door opened and in walked Bud. He had the hood of his parka pulled tightly over his head.

"You here to give your statements?" he asked as he unzipped the jacket.

"I'm finished with mine," said Lindsay.

Just then, Jennifer walked out with Vasquez.

"You're next, Cici," Vasquez announced.

Bud looked at his watch. "Do you mind if I go next, Cici? It's my Sunday to take up the offering at church." He looked over to Vasquez. "I mean, if it's alright with you."

Vasquez nodded. "Fine by me." Then he looked over to Cici.

"Me, too," she said.

"Before we start," said Bud. "Mac and Julie said they still want us to join them for the first night of Hanukkah tomorrow. They want to make it a celebration of Marley's life."

"I think that's a wonderful idea," said Jennifer.

Tameka reentered the room carrying a stack of papers. "What's a wonderful idea?" she asked.

"To share special memories of Marley at the Goldbergs' house tomorrow night," answered Bud.

"I hate to bring this up," said Vasquez. "But since Marley never married, it appears he has no living relatives...."

Cici smiled. "I'll take care of the funeral."

"The examiner's releasing the body on Wednesday morning," said Vasquez. "In his will Marley requested to be cremated."

"I'll pick up his ashes on Thursday morning," said Cici. "We'll have the service that afternoon."

"Christmas Day." Lindsay smiled. "Marley was the perfect blend of love and peace and an inspiration to all; we can sprinkle his ashes by the lake at his house."

"We'll combine all our holidays," said Bud. "Hanukkah begins Monday, Christmas Day is Thursday, and Kwanzaa begins on Friday."

"When everybody comes to my dance class's performance on Friday for the first night of Kwanzaa, we'll toast special libations to Marley," said Tameka.

"To borrow a word from Sir Richard Branson," said a smiling Tym, "we'll celebrate a Happy Chrismahanukwanzakah."

"I can't think of a better send-off," said Cici.

* * *

On Monday evening, just after sundown, Bud, Lindsay, Sheriff Vasquez and his wife, Deputy Tym, Tameka and her son, Cici, and the other members of the Lawtonville Arts Guild met at the Goldbergs.

"Where's Jennifer?" asked Mac as he set the Menorah on the windowsill and inserted two candles, one in the middle and another at the far right.

Cici looked at her watch. "She said she was coming when I spoke to her earlier today."

At that moment the front door squeaked open and Jennifer's head appeared. "Sorry." She had a fresh bandage on her other arm.

"What happened now?" asked Lindsay.

"Butler woke up limping, so I tried to hold him down to see if I could find anything stuck in his paw," grumbled Jennifer. "He shot out the door. That's why I'm late: because I've been riding around looking for him."

"Oh, I hope he'll be okay," said Tameka.

"It's the woodland creatures I pity," chipped in Jennifer.

"Everyone ready?" asked Julie.

All conversation stopped while Mac lit the middle candle and repeated three blessings. Then he picked up the Shamash and lit the other candle for the first night of Hanukkah.

Julie opened her arms. "The food is on the table."

"Marley always was the first in line for the latkes," said Tameka as she placed scoops of applesauce and sour cream on her son's plate. "It just doesn't seem right."

Lindsay focused her attention on Vasquez. "What's the latest?"

"It's still pretty sketchy," he said. "So far nothing out of the ordinary has shown up."

"Do they think the killer could be from out of town?" asked Bud.

Vasquez shook his head no. "The only prints they've lifted are from you." He waved a finger toward Cici, Bud, Lindsay, and Julie.

The four slowed their chewing, looking as if they were being served their last meal.

"Well, they sure cleaned up outside his house," said Jennifer. "I stopped by there to see if Butler might have run back home." She took a fried doughnut. "The area where he lay was picked clean... not even a piece of the pot was left."

"Butler wasn't there?" asked Cici.

"Uh-huh," said Jennifer. "But I didn't go inside or cross the yellow tape." She sighed. "I don't think I'll ever be able to go in Marley's cabin again."

"Marley was the best," said Lindsay.

"The kindest," added Bud.

Everyone shared stories about Marley, acting like it was a normal holiday celebration, but thoughts of "who?" danced in their heads.

* * *

On December 25th the same group assembled at Marley's house to sprinkle his ashes.

"Where'd you get this urn?" groaned Bud as held the container with Marley's remains.

"It was one I had in my garage," answered Cici. "Found it at the flea market last spring."

"I hope the service isn't too long." Bud shifted the urn to get a tighter grip.

"Why don't you set it on the porch railing?" suggested Lindsay. "See, there's the stain where the flower pot used to be."

Jennifer grimaced at the stain, but no one else seemed to think anything odd about the idea.

After the urn was positioned securely, the group listened to the minister from Marley's church read from the Bible. After he finished the scripture, each person contributed a sentiment.

"Let's join hands," said Reverend Miller, "and honor Marley Jones with a moment of silence."

Hands joined, heads bowed, and silence settled over the circle.

A soft mewling poked the quiet.

"Did you hear that?" asked Cici.

The mewling became louder.

"It sounded like it came from under the porch," said Vasquez.

Deputy Tym crouched on all fours and inched forward. From beneath the porch came a muffled, "It's a kitten."

Suddenly the little door from the kitchen slammed open and an explosion of fur and yowls screeched onto the railing. The massive body of the Maine Coon cat careened into the urn and sent it sailing downward onto Tym's foot.

To a background of screaming and crying, Cici muttered, "Butler did it?"

* * *

After the dance performance for Kwanzaa, the audience met in the main room at the Arts Center for refreshments.

"While it doesn't change the fact that Marley's dead," said Bud, "I sure feel better that it was an accident."

"Talk about a freaky way to go." Julie shuddered.

Vasquez nodded. "The crime lab report proved

that the piece of pottery imbedded in Butler's paw matched the one that killed Marley. They even found four paw prints on the pot."

"So, Marley sat down at his desk, heard the kitten, and—" started Mac.

"And the rest of the scenario played out before our eyes at his funeral," finished Julie.

"Now I have Butler," said Jennifer, "and the new kitten, O'Hara."

"Named after Scarlet, of course." Cici laughed.

Tym hobbled up, his left foot in a cast. "Broken ankle is the final verdict."

"Well, we're certainly glad you didn't succumb to the same fate as poor Marley," said Jennifer.

"I'm a lucky man, all right," he said. He leaned into his crutch.

"Don't you dare say it," cautioned Vasquez.

A wide grin spread across his face as Deputy Tym said, "God bless us, everyone!"

Copyright © 2008 Janice Alonso

Just Call Me Nick

Terrie Farley Moran

It ain't every day a guy in a Santa suit pulls up to the pump in a big red Woodie wagon with deer antlers stuck above each headlight and sleigh runners bolted to the fenders. Forget the Chevy Silverados and Dodge Rams with puny wreaths hanging from the grill. The Woodie left them in the holiday decorating dust. Even for mid-December it was an unusual sight, and this year a scary one. Over the last couple of weeks, half a dozen gas stations in the north part of the county were held up by a shotgun toting Santa, evil enough to knock two teeth right out of the mouth of the night guy at a small double pump near Manorville.

When I caught sight of Santa and his sleigh I was inside making change for a couple of airheads who were passing a joint back and forth in a silver Beetle. Through a clearing in the green-tinted glass wax Christmas trees scattered on the office window, I could see Elvin pumping a red mustang, one of the few that didn't have a young and pretty girl behind the wheel. Her daddy must have borrowed the car.

Our hang-out buddies Joe and Corey had their leather jackets zipped against the snappy wind gusting down from the hills up-road. They were having one of their regular battles. Was Bruce Springsteen's *Born to Run* the best album of 1975 or did the Eagles outdo the Boss with *One of These Nights*?

The two of them sat next to the soda machine

on creaky wooden chairs leaned back against the wall. They had no idea how much they looked like a couple of old farts in a cowboy movie. You know, the toothless gray beards playing checkers in front of the general store.

I kept stock still, hoping Santa wouldn't notice me through the window. I wanted to stay near the phone, just in case. Santa stepped out of the Woodie without a shotgun. I let out a short sigh of relief but wasn't ready to walk away from the telephone. I watched Santa rock back and forth. His calf high boots, a leather match to his shiny black belt, rolled from toe to heel and back. Then he swung his arms, loosening his shoulders until I thought the seams would burst the sleeves right off his red plush jacket. Truth be told, the jacket was snug around the belly. Either the guy in the costume store gave him the wrong size suit, or his pillow was too big. He looked around, saw the sign with the arrow and headed to the men's room. Elvin and the man in the Mustang both watched him. I guess they were wondering, same as me.

Joe and Corey, still arguing about record albums, never saw him coming 'til he walked right past them. Corey flopped his chair with a thud and called after him.

"Hey Santa, don't forget my address come Christmas."

Santa let out a deep throated, "Ho, Ho" and disappeared around the side of the building before the third "Ho" was out of his mouth.

I left the office, gave the Beetle her change and waited for an old man with a lumpy black hat pulled down clear past his eyebrows to stop his ancient Buick at the pump. He kept easing back and forth until he got the car exactly where he wanted, about an inch from where it landed on his first try. Sure enough, the old guy wanted three gallons of regular, little more than a dollar's worth. Elvin and me had talked about it more than once. We're thinking the geezers just don't want to drop dead with a full tank of gas in the car. They want that couple of dollars to be in the bank where it could help pay for a nice funeral down at Morton's with a big stand of flowers from Delsey's.

I handed the old guy in the Buick his change and took two steps back so he didn't catch my toes with his rear tire. Then I heard Joe squeal like a pig followed by a chair thump. Then the second chair thumped.

Before I got a chance to see what stirred up doofus and doofus, Elvin called to me, his voice all serious-like. I turned his way. A Ford pickup, been knocked around some, was in the Mustang's spot. It took a second for me to register a guy wearing a bright red sweatshirt and a Santa mask holding a double barrel shotgun on Elvin. Santa motioned with the shotgun for me to move over by Joe and Corey. He gave Elvin a head nod in the same direction.

What are the odds on two Santas?

I gave a side glance at the Woodie. Empty.

Shotgun Santa growled at me. "Get over here, buddy."

I raised my hands and over I got. I didn't want to give away that there was anyone else around, so I didn't peek at the corner that turned to the rest rooms. I hoped Woodie Santa would sneak a quick look around the side of the building, and figure out how to get us some help. For his part, Shotgun Santa didn't seem to notice the Woodie. Or if he did, he must have figured it was some kind of Christmas decoration.

Once Shotgun Santa had us in a herd, he sent me in the office to empty the cash register. His directions were real clear.

"Go inside and rip the phone cord. Toss the phone out here. Then go empty the register into this. I want the change, too. Right down to the pennies."

He pushed a tattered half-barrel sized feed sack at me. How much money did he think we had on hand? This wasn't the Horn Dog Saloon at closing time on a Saturday night.

I stepped toward the office door thinking it didn't seem right somehow. There was four of us and only one of him. We should be able to take him. Then again, he was the one with the shotgun.

There was nothing else to be done. I yanked the phone cord clean out of the wall and chucked the phone through the doorway. It crashed when it hit the concrete. The heavy black shell of the phone cracked like a split in lake ice in early spring. I stood in the doorway and watched a chunk of it drop away from the metal innards.

Shotgun Santa hurried me with a shout. "Get my

money and move on out here, boy."

I watched him give a poke with the shotgun right into Elvin's stomach to remind me he was serious. As I turned back inside the office I let my eyes sweep the road, hoping for a distraction. Maybe a couple of cars looking for a few dollars worth of gas. I pretty much had given up on Woodie Santa. He either died in the men's room or he saw what a mess we had and ducked for cover.

I popped the register and shook my head. Shotgun Santa was going to be mighty let down by the lone ten dollar bill hanging out with a few fives and a bunch of singles. Wouldn't cover even the bottom of the feed sack. I dropped a fistful of bills and change into the bag and walked to the door, thinking we might as well get this over before someone gets hurt.

I opened the door, and stepped down. My mouth dropped and my eyes bugged. Shotgun Santa had grown a second head.

His first head was looking at the feed sack like it held all the gold from Fort Knox, so he missed seeing my surprise. The shotgun in his right hand sagged an inch or more as soon as he dropped his left hand off the barrel to reach for the feed sack. When he took that small move forward, his second head stayed behind.

Woodie Santa.

He swung his wide black belt in a generous circle over his head, the buckle aimed right at Shotgun Santa. I ducked to the left, figuring when the buckle struck, it would set off at least one barrel, blowing some part of me to hell and back. The buckle landed, slamming Shotgun Santa's knuckles. The long gun danced from his hand, bounced off the edge of the soda machine and spun along the floor.

I pitched myself flat and put my hands over my ears but that shotgun never did throw a shell.

Shotgun Santa gave a halfhearted grab at his double barrel but I recovered enough to push it out of reach. Joe and Elvin grabbed his arms, and we all started whaling on him. Then we pushed him down into Corey's chair and stood semi-circle in front of him. Elvin was bold enough to pull off his mask. Not anyone I'd seen before, or wanted to see again.

Woodie Santa, his belt once again around his chubby waist, had picked up the shotgun. He had it cradled in one arm like a hunter going out for deer. Well, in his case, maybe not deer.

I took my first close look. Woodie Santa had a real beard. It was wiry. Not at all like those cotton candy beards for sale at Woolworth's. Around his eyes and nose he had the kind of wrinkles my grandma has— lines that shift and roll with every word and deepen whenever she laughs.

"If that's your only phone, one of you is going to have to ride down the road to call the sheriff to come pick up this faker." He turned to the used-to-be Shotgun Santa.

"Where did you come up with that silly Santa mask? Don't you know what a real Santa looks like?" Woodie Santa puffed out his chest, impossible as that seemed to be.

"You trashed my reputation. You trashed the

reputation of Santas everywhere. What are the children of the world supposed to think when they hear that Santa Claus hit some young guy in Manorville across the face with the stock of a shotgun?"

"Is this the gun?" Woodie Santa raised the shotgun over his head and brought it down in a slow arc inching closer to our prisoner whose face, turning a sickly green, was starting to clash with his red sweatshirt.

Woodie Santa pulled the gun back.

"You're lucky I'm a peaceful man. Wouldn't hurt a fly."

At the sound of that, Sweatshirt Santa couldn't help but look at the welts on his fingers from Woodie Santa's belt buckle.

"Well, time to go. It's my busy season, you know. I'll just take this shotgun so it won't be causing any more trouble and I'll trust you boys to get that copycat into the hands of the law so that he won't be causing any more trouble either."

We all started talking at once.

"Thank you."

"Thanks for the rescue."

"Hey, best Christmas present ever, man."

I stuck out my hand and Woodie and I shook.

"Thank you Santa, uh, Mr. Claus."

He crinkled his nose and all those lines and wrinkles slid to new places.

"Pleasure to help out, son. You just call me Nick."

Like we was buddies.

We all watched the sleigh peel onto route seventeen. I half expected to see it rise up and glide over the tree tops.

Corey was the first to almost say it out loud.

"Do you think... he...?"

We stood quiet for a full minute or more, no one brave enough to say "Yep, that was Santa all right."

Finally I said, "His name is Nick. He said to call him Nick."

Everyone nodded, relieved to put a name on the guy, and we turned our attention back to Sweatshirt Santa. We decided that Elvin would run down the road to the Lansky's farm and call the sheriff. Joe and Corey would stand over the prisoner, while I'd tend the station.

I gathered the pieces of the telephone and put them on the front step. Then I saw the feed sack lying where I'd dropped it in the scuffle.

I reached in to get the money, figuring I'd need change for the next customer. The bag was empty. I ran my arm to the bottom twice more with the same result. I crawled all around looking under and over every piece of gear spread around the gas station. I found two pennies and a nickel but they were dusty, probably been laying there for months.

I walked over to the others, dragging the bag along. I threw it in Sweatshirt Santa's lap.

"You took our money. Where is it? Get up so I can search you."

Joey looked at me.

"How could he? We got him first. He never got

his hands on the bag."

Corey nodded. "The money must have fell out."

"Nah, I looked everywhere, under the steps, behind the gas cans, even under the soda machine. The money is gone."

Sweatshirt Santa burst out laughing, like he couldn't hold it in another minute.

"You chumps. He actually had you believing he was the real deal. Santa Claus, my aunt Fanny. Santa thief is more like it. While you dopes were hassling me, I was watching Santa empty the sack and pocket the money."

He stopped to take a breath and wipe his nose on his sleeve.

"I'm a copycat, okay. But I was copycatting a thief dressed like Santa, not the real thing. There is no real thing. This was my second job. I did Manorville and you guys. He musta done the rest. You boys are dumber than dumb."

Dumbstruck's more like it. While I watched the sheriff's car coming down route seventeen, I couldn't figure what I'd say. My mind was caught on me shaking hands with Woodie Santa and him saying, "Just call me Nick."

Copyright © Terrie Farley Moran

The Longest Night

S. M Harding

Mairead Hannay blew out a long breath and watched it crystallize on the cold mountain air. Standing on the porch of the old lodge, she gazed out over the Chama Valley spread below, snow-covered and dazzling in the bright sunshine. Dark-bellied clouds were massing on the far horizon. *Snow coming. Hope the clan arrives before the storm. We're still here, Fergus. Two hundred years and counting, keeping the old ways like you taught your wife when you brought her here from the Highlands. These mountains reminded you of home and now they're home to your clan.*

She was about to turn and go inside when she saw her brother's truck bouncing up the frozen ruts of the road. She waited until he pulled into the yard. "Sheep OK?"

"All bedded down and waiting for the storm, Meg," Rabbie said. "Left the dogs with them, but coyotes with any sense will be denning tonight. Your end done?"

"Bannock cakes and black buns cooling, Yule log duly decorated, ashes cleaned from the fireplace, house cleaned, and Cailleach Nallaich carved," she said, ticking off items on her fingers. "I forget anything?"

"The Laphraig and Glenfiddich?"

She nodded. "And the Bowmore 17. You know Andrew won't drink anything but. And Elspeth likes it, too."

"I wonder how many more winter solstices we'll have her. She must be close to ninety. Last of that generation to celebrate all the old ways."

"She's ninety-two," Meg said. "And not slowing down one bit. I wonder if she'll let Catriona drive."

"Which great-granddaughter is that?"

"Iona's. The black sheep in our herd of white-faced." She grinned.

Rabbie turned to the mountain that loomed over the lodge. "Already Old Scotsman is misting over. Bitter cold tonight on top of the snow."

* * *

Meg opened the door to Elspeth Hannay's arrival as the sun slanted toward the western horizon. She gave the white-haired woman a cautious hug, then stood aside to let her in.

Elspeth took the arm of the woman standing behind her and pulled her forward. "This is Catriona Ruiz, my great-granddaughter."

"Call me Cat. People could never get the pronunciation right, always wanted to put the 'o' in, so I shortened it," said the young woman, unwrapping her Campbell tartan scarf.

Meg took their coats and settled them before the monster cast-iron stove in the small parlor. "Can I get you anything?"

"A wee dram would be most appreciated," Elspeth said, taking off her tam and setting it on the table beside her.

Wee dram, cute. Normally there was only a trace of a burr in Elspeth's 'r's'. She must be putting on a show for Cat. I wonder why? She poured the scotch and handed it to Elspeth. "And you?"

"You have soda?" Cat asked. "I don't really drink hard liquor because it interferes with my psychic abilities. It's a garden to be tended, you know."

"Meg, you know the second sight runs in the family," Elspeth said. "Your own mother had a clear ability which you've always chosen to ignore."

I'm not going another round with Elspeth over second sight, particularly not when the clan's gathering. "Rabbie and Lucia don't allow their children to drink soda pop, so we don't have any in the house. But we do have spring water. From our own spring, up the mountain a bit."

I went to get her water and when I came back, Elspeth was explaining that Lucia and the children were at her pueblo for their own solstice rituals. As I handed it to Cat, I examined her face for a family resemblance. I found it in her dark eyes, almost as black as pitch. That and the jaw line, a stubborn jut forward.

"Grams hasn't told me much about the ritual," she said. "Will it be like a Wiccan one? Although I don't suppose we'll being doing it skyclad in this weather."

Elspeth chuckled at the confusion on my face. "Meg, you're going to have to get out more. Wicca is one of the Neo-Pagan movements. Looks back to

England and Ireland for old wisdom. Lots of spells and magic."

"No, no spells, no magic. Just a clan remembering roots and welcoming in the new year. We'll have dinner tonight, light the Yule log, then greet the sun in the morning."

"Metaphorically if the weather forecast holds," Elspeth said. "In Scotland when the first Fergus left, the people celebrated Hogmanay at the time of winter solstice. The idea is to clean out the residue of the old year and welcome the new. Besides certain foods, one of the traditions was 'first footing,' which foretold the luck of the household for the new year."

"Except we've lived in such a remote place, the first visitor never came until the year was half over," Meg said. "So we never paid much attention to that part."

Elspeth gave Meg a fierce look. "The tradition goes back to the time those Vikings were raiding. The first visitor to cross the threshold after midnight was thought to bring bad luck if he was fair, blonde and blue-eyed. But if he was dark, like a proper Scotsman, he brought good luck."

"I find giving the house a good cleaning midwinter a better tradition," Meg said. "Our ancestors were nothing but practical folk. Kept away the pestilence."

"And you burned juniper when you'd finished the cleaning, I bet," Elspeth challenged. "And why did you do that?"

"Makes everything smell fresh."

"Pshaw. Drives out the evil spirits and cleanses the soul of the place." She crossed her arms. "You carved Cailleach Nallaich."

Meg nodded, crossed her own arms.

Elspeth turned to Cat. "The Old Wife represents the evils of winter. She's the hag who brings death. Burning her on the Yule fire protects the occupants of the household from death."

They heard another car laboring up the drive, then a door slam. Meg welcomed Andrew, a tall man with a close-trimmed black beard. "Let me stow my bags in my room," he said and took the broad stairs two at a time.

When he returned, she led him into the parlor and introduced him to Cat.

"Andrew Hannay, pillar of the Taos literary establishment," she said. Not pausing to ask, she poured a tumbler of Bowmore and handed it to him.

He stood before the stove, shoulders hunched. "I wanted to beat the storm over the mountain. Going to be a wild night."

"*You're* the novelist? *Bright Dawn* and the Hollister family saga?"

"Guilty," he said with a slight bow.

"Oh, they're wonderful. Is there a new novel coming out soon?"

He shrugged. "Where's Rabbie?"

"Cleaning up from bedding down the sheep."

"Ah, what would we do without those beautiful Cheviot?"

"Starve," Meg said.

"Cheviot? Don't you have Merino?" asked Cat.

"Merino are Spanish. The second Fergus imported our own white-faced herd from the Highlands," Meg said. "Good and sturdy, used to climbing which, he claimed, the Merino weren't."

"Hello, everyone," said Rabbie, as he walked into the room tucking in the tail of his flannel shirt.

"Is that the Hannay tartan?" Cat asked.

"No," Rabbie answered. "L. L. Bean catalogue. Part of our clan belongs to the Lowland branch down in Dumfries. I'd be wearing Campbell."

"Our ancestors were pledged to the Campbells and so wore their tartan," Elspeth said. "But we kept the clan name. Always were a stiff-necked bunch of ruffians."

"Seumas still not here?" Rabbie asked.

"Lives the closest, probably isn't worried about the snow," Meg answered.

"Well, he better hurry. The first flakes are coming down now."

The smell of roast lamb drove Andrew to pacing. "Must we wait for Seumas?"

"The roast should be ready and I don't want it to dry out waiting for him to make his entrance," Meg said, rising. "If Seumas is here by the time it's on the table, fine. If not, it's his bad fortune."

She was just setting the last platter on the table when they heard the knocking on the front door. Rabbie got up to answer it and they heard male voices and stamping in the hall.

A short, portly man with eyes the color of

coffee and sandy hair entered the dining room, straightening his formal jacket and kilt of light blue and yellow Hannay plaid. He nodded to the rest, scanned the dishes on the table, and took the empty seat. "Carve, Rabbie, I'm starved. Snow came out of nowhere and I had business to finish in Chama."

"And what might that business be?" Andrew asked.

Seumas gave him a steely look across the table. "Real estate—what else? Boom time in the valley, and about time. Can't be one decrepit narrow gauge train, sheep and cattle forever."

"All those people from California moving here with too much money for their own good," Meg said. *Keep quiet, woman. Already enough tension at the table. Andrew's got something on his mind, been antsy since he got here. He's looking daggers back at Seumas.* "Let go ahead and start the Colecannon from this end."

They circulated the side dishes, then the platter of thick-sliced lamb. Conversation ceased, which Meg thought was a blessing. She noticed Cat grabbing quick glances at Seumas through half-closed eyes. Elspeth's glances were divided between Andrew and Seumas. Rabbie kept his gaze on his plate, and Seumas ate his methodical way through large portions of everything. Andrew dutifully tasted everything but ate little, Meg thought, as if he was replaying an ancient battle in his mind.

She was relieved when Rabbie rose and led them into the sitting room where the fireplace was clean, a fire laid in preparation for the Yule log. They could hear the wind moaning through the flue. The room was chilly and Meg checked the eight-day clock on the stone mantel. *Less than half an hour until we can light it, just enough time for Elspeth to tell the family saga.* She watched Rabbie seat Elspeth, then walk to the window. She wondered if he could see more than the whiteout that was apparent to her.

"After the Slaughter of Inverlochy in February of 1645, Fergus Hannay was left with nothing but a wife who was pregnant with their first child . . ." Elspeth began.

Meg knew the story, word for word. Weary from the blood and war, they traveled over the North Atlantic. Fergus's longing for mountains without politics kept the family moving westward from New York to Tennessee to New Mexico.

Her thoughts drifted to the tensions at the table tonight. Seumas and Andrew had never gotten along. Seamus called him a romantic who had no idea about the reality of working the land; Andrew responded by accusing Seumas of being more concerned about owning the land than working it. Or loving it. *That's us. Always going on about the land. Seeing beauty or work, never both at the same time. Divided like the Scots themselves. Highland and Lowland. The bard and the logician.*

". . . and when Fergus saw this land, he knew he'd found home again. He bargained with the local natives, then the Spanish, settled his family here. And here our hearts have their center ever since,"

Elspeth finished.

Finished wool-gathering just in time. She rose, as did Rabbie. The fire blazed from both ends, met in the center. Meg picked up one end of the Yule log, Rabbie the other. Carefully, they lowered it onto the fire. The pine and juniper sprigs that decorated it caught immediately and spat as they burned.

Rabbie rolled the drink cart before the fireplace and poured a shot for everyone, according to their taste. Meg had remembered to put a tumbler of spring water with the scotch. When each was standing, Meg offered a thanksgiving for the bounty and beauty of the land in the year past and Rabbie gave a toast to the new year and the turning of the seasons. They raised their glasses and drank.

Pounding reverberated through the house.

"Who could be at the front door in weather like this?" Meg asked.

"Likely a stranded traveler, though he must be daft to be out tonight," Rabbie said. He set down his glass and walked into the hall. The others crowded after him.

They opened the door to a man covered from head to toe in snow. Rabbie pulled him in, shut the door to the raging blizzard.

The snowman began to shake the snow off his sheepskin jacket and watch cap. "Thank God you had your lights on this late. Ran my truck into a snowbank. Snow so thick you can't even see to the end of the hood."

Rabbie took his jacket and cap and Meg

bustled him into the sitting room to stand in front of the fire. Steam rose off his pants and formed a halo above his head. "Name's Gus. I'm a deputy sheriff and was trying to get everyone down off the mountain and the gate across the road closed. Had to wait for the last fool over."

"I'll get you some coffee," Meg said. "Have you eaten?"

"No, ma'am, I haven't and would surely appreciate it. But is that scotch? A wee dram would hit the spot right now."

Meg hurried to the kitchen and when she turned to reach for a tray, bumped into Elspeth.

"Good fortune this year, a dark one has passed the threshold first."

"I hadn't thought about that," Meg replied.

"You also didn't think about the Cailleach Nallaich."

"You're right. I'll do it when I take the tray in."

"It's too late for protection. Got to keep your wits about you, girl, or you invite death." Elspeth pulled her shawl closer. "What time is sunrise?"

"A little after eight, but I'll have coffee on at six."

"Good, good. I'm going on up to bed, lass, glad to have a warm, sturdy shelter on a night like this."

Rabbie and the other males seemed intent on staying up the longest, sipping and trading war stories. Meg escorted Cat upstairs and showed her to the guest room. "It should stay pretty warm, we have passive solar heating, but if you get cold, there's a fire laid in the stove."

Cat turned, looking around the room. "This is wonderful."

"Come back next year, and we'll make it yours."

A faint cloud crossed her face. "My mother would kill me if she knew I was up here at all, much less with Grams."

"Ah, well."

"Uh, Meg, I gather you don't think much about the second sight, but I can see things. Please tell Andrew to be careful."

"Why?"

Another cloud passed, this one darker. "He's going to die soon."

Meg shivered. *This room is drafty.*

"And another thing. That's the first Fergus in the painting above the mantel?" Meg nodded. "Did you notice how much the deputy resembles him?"

"No, but I was more concerned with warming up the poor man. I'll ring the breakfast bell at seven. Sleep tight."

* * *

Meg awoke at her normal 5:30 and looked out the window by her bed. An almost full moon illuminated the absolutely silent scene and etched it in brilliant white and stark black shadows.

Storm's over, but I bet we got over a foot of snow. Way to Santa Fe and Chama should be open, but Andrew's going to have to stay. Maybe he'd be safest here, among family. She shivered. *Strange creature, Cat. Second sight. Good Lord, save us from psychics.*

She showered and dressed, quietly went downstairs to start the day. The coffee maker was spluttering and sending up clouds of aroma when Rabbie walked in yawning.

"Strange, last night. Our first footing and how much he looks like the first Fergus. Especially in the eyes. And I thought Andrew was going to challenge Seumas to daggers at forty feet."

"Did you get a chance to talk to Andrew alone?"

"Seumas stuck like a Hound Tongue's burr." He leaned against the counter, crossed his arms. "It was late when I got them to bed. I put Gus at the end of the hall."

"I didn't air out that room or change the linens. What will he think of us?"

"Any port in a storm. I imagine he's grateful not to be sleeping in a snowbank. They'll be up in a bit, so I'll get the fire in the sitting room going. Blessed Solstice, Meg."

"And to you, brother."

He returned not two minutes later. "It's Andrew—he's dead!"

"No! Dead? Are you sure?"

"His body's cold, Meg. Is the phone still out?"

She put the receiver to her ear and nodded. "No cell phone signal out here and they won't get a plow this far today. What are we going to do?"

"Rouse our dark visitor."

* * *

Gus bent over the body for a long time, then rose. He scanned the area around the body, pulled a handkerchief from his pocket, and picked up a glass with it. He swirled the dregs, sniffed. "You have rat poison around here?"

"D-Con," Meg answered. We get packrats every fall. You don't think . . ."

"He bled from the nose and mouth, this scotch smells foul. What would you think?"

"I wouldn't be thinking about rat poison."

"Did he have heart problems? He might have been on a blood thinner."

"He never said anything." She glanced at Rabbie and he shook his head.

Gus put down the glass and signaled them to leave the room. "You have a key for this room?"

Meg hurried down the hall to a long table by the staircase, opened the drawer, and took out a key ring. She flipped through the keys as she walked back, picked one, and locked the door. Gus took the key ring and went up the staircase.

"Oh, Rabbie, Andrew!"

He gave her a big hug. They stood that way, rocking slightly, until Gus returned. "No prescription medicine, but I found an interesting thing in this." He held up a black leather briefcase. "It's his?"

"Yes, I remember it from when he arrived. Instead of piling his bags in the hall with the others, he took them directly up to his room."

Gus nodded. "I'd be most grateful for a cup of

coffee."

When they were seated at the kitchen table, Rabbie looked at Gus. "You think someone in this house poisoned him last night. Who? Why?"

Gus put the briefcase on the table, snapped the locks, and pulled a sheaf of papers from it. He pushed them toward Meg. "Do you recognize this?"

She scanned the first sheet, flipped through the others. "I don't understand."

Rabbie moved his chair next to Meg. "My God! Andrew was selling this land out from under us. How could he?"

"Not Andrew," she said, flipping to the back page. "Look."

"Dumfries Development Corporation? Dumfries?"

"The Lowland Hannay clan. Short, stout, shopkeepers and government officials. Who wear the Hannay tartan, not the Campbell. Ring any bells, Brother?"

"Seumas? And how can he buy this land when it's not for sale?"

"We evidently signed this." She pointed to two signatures at the bottom of the page.

"What a bastard! All that talk of his about a ski resort—he was going to put it here."

"Where's the rat poison?" Gus asked.

"Pantry," Meg said, starting to rise.

"I'll get it. Baggie?"

"In the pantry, too."

Gus went into the panty, returned with the

poison in the baggie. "I think I have enough to warrant escorting Seumas Hannay to the station for questioning. I'll send the investigators out as soon as I get there."

Gus hustled a loudly protesting and handcuffed Seumas out the door shortly after. He turned to Rabbie and Meg. "Thank you for taking in a stranger. I have four-wheel drive, so now I can see where I'm going, I don't need you kind folk to dig me out." He pushed Seumas ahead of him, then turned. "Don't forget to greet the sun today."

When Elspeth and Cat joined them in the kitchen, Meg tried to break the news gently.

Elspeth wailed. "Andrew never drinks Laphraig. Why did he start last night?"

Meg and Rabbie exchanged a quick glance.

"The Bowmore was gone," Rabbie said. "We finished it after you went upstairs."

"No, no, no."

"You didn't – "

"Don't say a word, Grams," Cat said. "She's shocked daft, doesn't know what she's saying. But where are Seumas and Fergus? Seumas is behind whatever's going on."

"Fergus?"

"Uh, Gus."

Meg gave her a long, steady stare but couldn't divine what was going on behind those dark eyes. She told them what Gus had done and that he was sending the sheriff's people back to the crime scene.

A soft ray of sunlight passed through the

window and touched Elspeth's cheek. She stood. "We must greet the sun, for Andrew."

* * *

They'd finished the old ritual when the sheriff plowed up the driveway with the crime scene van following. The men shepherded the clan into the parlor and stationed a deputy with them. They saw a gurney pass by the door and the sheriff motioned for Meg and Rabbie.

"Thanks for calling, Rabbie. Surprised your phone's working."

"I didn't call and our phone's been dead since the storm hit last night. Didn't Gus bring Seumas into the station?"

"Gus?"

"Your deputy," Meg said. "He was stranded last night, came right after midnight."

"I don't have a deputy named Gus. Last name?"

They glanced at each other. "He didn't say." Rabbie told the sheriff what had happened last night and what had followed his discovery of the body.

"So the prime suspect has disappeared along with important evidence, both under the escort of a deputy who isn't. Damnest story I've ever heard." He reset his Stetson on his head. "And the key was in the lock."

"But we saw him pocket the whole ring. It wasn't in the lock when he left," Meg said.

The sheriff shrugged. "Right now, we'll proceed with the investigation. My guess is Seumas had his accomplice cart him off before we got here. State police have been investigating his business dealings for the past six months. He was in deep trouble. But just in case, please tell your guests not to leave until we release them."

* * *

The group settled around the stove in the parlor that night after dinner. Elspeth had been silent all day, had barely touched her food. Cat hovered around the woman, anticipating any need.

"I did it, you know," Elspeth said after a long silence. "Andrew called me and told me what he'd found. He was going to confront Seumas this morning, turn him over to the authorities. But I believe in the old clan justice. I should have let Andrew handle it the way he wanted. Dear God, I'm sorry."

"This isn't Scotland, dear," Meg said. "It's a new country with different ways. Though I'm not sure your way, had it worked, wouldn't have been better. Seumas wouldn't have escaped."

"Seumas didn't escape," Cat said. "I can't believe you people! You've been raised in this tradition, on this land, your whole life. And yet you can't see what's in front of your face."

"I beg your pardon," Rabbie said.

"I've had second sight as long as I can remember, but until I finally met Grams, my parents thought I was psychotic. Grams taught me how to use it, control it."

"What does that have to do with Seumas

escaping?" Meg asked.

"Gus. The ghost of the first Fergus, come to save the land and wreak vengeance on the clansman who betrayed us."

"Ghost."

Elspeth nodded. "He kept wavering. My sight may be fading, but I knew. And still couldn't keep my temper in check. You never burned the Cailleach Nallaich. I took that as a sign."

"Good Lord," Meg said. "Your fingerprints must have been on the D-Con, but without the box and the main suspect, there's no way to prove you did anything." *Elspeth can live out her life free, our land is safe. Our dark visitor did bring us good luck. But at such cost.*

Copyright © 2008 S. M. Harding

In the Nick of Time

Gayle Bartos-Pool

"Is he dead?"

"If he isn't, the cold will finish him off. Go through his pockets."

"Why do I have to do it?"

"You're the junior partner," said Vinnie while he tugged the ski jacket around his ample belly. He tried it on at a local ski shop and then walked out the door with it. The security tag was still attached, but he cut it off, taking a walnut size piece of cloth and padding with it.

"Since when did I get to be the junior partner?" said Larry. He was a foot shorter than his buddy, and stringy like an old chicken. "I'm the one who told you this place was a gold mine." He leaned down and tentatively rummaged through the man's pockets. He didn't want to get too friendly, but he could hear the jingle of loose change. He jammed his hand into the front pocket and came back with a fist full of coins.

"Get his wallet," said Vinnie, reaching out and taking the money.

"I'll have to roll him over," said Larry, straightening and giving an involuntary shiver. An icy gust stung his eyes, the only exposed skin under his ski mask.

"He won't care. Just do it."

"When do I get to be an equal partner?"

mumbled Larry. "This was my idea."

"You saw an ad on the bus about skiing with the rich and famous and thought we might score big-time up here. I'm the one who thought about hitchhiking to this godforsaken place. I paid for the hotel room. And you don't even know how to ski."

"And I suppose you do?"

"Just roll him over."

"I need help," said Larry, still not wanting to kneel down near the body.

"Get your hands under him and lift. Gravity will do the rest."

Larry sighed. He got down in the snow along the path and thought about it. "He looks heavy."

"Oh, for crying out loud."

Vinnie dropped heavily to his knees and got both his arms underneath the man's designer ski parka and lifted. Obviously the man lying in the snow wasn't all that heavy because he flipped over and rolled down the steep embankment easily. He had enough momentum to start a small avalanche, gathering snow as he rolled and rolled.

Twenty feet below the ridge the snowman came to an abrupt stop against a small stand of trees. The snowball exploded in a shower of flakes as both men looked on.

"Yep," said Larry. "Gravity works."

"Oh, shut up. Let's get down there and finish the job."

"At least he's off the road," said Larry.

"Somebody could have seen us." He yanked off his ski mask and stuffed it in his pocket. His shaggy brown hair stood up like a punk rocker's.

"It's lunchtime. All those snobs at the lodge are chowing down in the dining room."

"I could use something to eat myself," said Larry, hearing his stomach growl under the secondhand jacket he wore. It was one of Vinnie's hand-me-downs. He was swimming in it. "I think I'll take his scarf. I'm freezing."

"And somebody sees you wearing it and recognizes it. No way. You can buy yourself a new one with the loot we'll make."

Larry sighed again. "How are we gonna get down there?"

Vinnie checked out the road. There was no easy way to access the narrow valley below them from the ridge road. "You go down. Slide on your butt if you have too."

"Me?"

"This was your brilliant idea. Get going."

Larry harrumphed. "Next time I hope I see a picture of the beach."

He stumbled down the side of the hill, going knee deep in snow that had been shot over the edge by a county snow blower. He finally got to the body and stood there with his hands on his skinny hips.

"Now what?" yelled Vinnie.

"He landed on his back." Larry stared at the neatly cropped salt and pepper beard on the man's face. It was now full of snow, and icicles were forming along the jaw line.

"Roll him over."

Larry tugged at the guy's jacket and managed to get the body to cooperate. He reached for the man's back pocket when he heard Vinnie yelling. "Duck! Duck!"

Larry looked up into the sky but didn't see anything.

"Somebody's coming, you idiot," shouted Vinnie. "Get out of sight."

Larry dived into the snow beside the guy in the red parka. He burrowed down as far as he could go and covered his head. Only his rear end was sticking up.

Vinnie started walking casually along the road like he had a reason to be there as the ski patrol vehicle drove up along side him and stopped.

"You okay, fella?" asked the ranger, rolling down the window. He looked like Dudley Do-Right, right down to the cleft in his chin and the full head of blond hair.

"Yeah. Just getting some exercise, if it's alright with you." Vinnie knew that last part sounded snarky, but he couldn't help himself.

"You got a car someplace?"

"I walked out here. I'll walk back."

The ranger noticed Vinnie's nice jacket. "You staying at the lodge?"

Vinnie put his elbow over the hole in the side.

"Yeah. Great place."

"Okay. Merry Christmas, buddy."

"Dudley" rolled up his window and headed down the road. Vinnie waited until the vehicle was out of sight and then rushed back to the spot where Larry had climbed over. He gave his pal the all clear. When Larry finally struggled up the hill to the road, Vinnie put out his hand and Larry reached for it.

"No. The wallet. Give me the wallet." Larry handed it over. "Three hundred and sixty bucks," Vinnie said after he opened all the little flaps. "Three hundred and sixty lousy bucks. That's all he had on him?" He looked at Larry with questioning eyes.

"I didn't take anything," He opened his jacket and dared his partner to search him. "Let's go back to the hotel. I'm cold and hungry."

They walked to the lodge. It was a long, frosty walk. Vinnie wouldn't speak to his pal. He gave Larry dirty looks the entire way. Larry squinted right back at him.

The men shared a small room at the rear of the four story hotel. It was the cheapest accommodation in the place. Vinnie made himself a cup of coffee with the in-room coffee maker while Larry took a hot shower and changed into drier pants. Then they headed for the dining room and something to eat.

The place was abuzz. The holiday crowd was usually boisterous, but this time they were uncommonly disturbed. A cluster of après-ski clad folks bunched around a large blond woman who had become very animated.

"My husband's out there in the snow and a blizzard's coming. What am I going to do?"

"Did he go with anyone, Mrs. Whitman?" asked a guy in a deep blue ski sweater.

"No. He went by himself along the upper road. He wanted to take a walk before lunch."

"What was he wearing?" asked a lady in a dove grey ski outfit.

"A red parka and a yellow and white scarf. His school colors."

Vinnie elbowed Larry. "See. I told you so."

"Gosh. I hope he was bundled up well enough to handle the weather," said another man. "That storm looks like a bad one." He shook his head.

"But he wasn't wearing gloves or a hat," said the worried wife. "Just that six-carat diamond on his hand. That won't keep him warm. Oh, what will I do? What will I do?"

"The rangers are out looking for him right now, Mrs. Whitman. Don't worry. They'll find him." The man in the blue sweater put his arm around the woman as the other people tried to console her.

Mrs. Whitman, her eyes wide with fear, looked up. "What will I tell the children? It's Christmas Eve. They'll want their father." She collapsed against the man next to her.

Larry had been watching the scene, biting his lower lip. "Gee. That's tough."

Vinnie pulled him off to the side. "We have to

go back."

"You're right. They need to know what happened to him."

"Not for the guy. For the diamond. Come on."

"I don't know," Larry said, holding back. "Look. Maybe we should just go get something to eat."

"Think about what we can buy after we sell that rock," said Vinnie, rubbing his hands together.

The pair headed out again on foot. The lodge provided snow boots, so they tramped along the road away from the warmth of the ski lodge and made their way to the location overlooking the valley below.

"What if we don't get back before the storm hits?" asked Larry.

"We've got plenty of time."

Larry looked up. The blue sky was turning purple and the breeze had picked up.

They found the spot where they had accidentally rolled the guy over the precipice.

"I don't see him," said Larry, straining to see into the pile of snow near the trees below.

"He's got to be there," said Vinnie, his voice anxious. "He's got to."

Vinnie charged over the edge. His weight had him sinking into the drifts up to his thighs. It was slow going, but finally they both got to the broken snowball that had entombed the man in the red parka.

"He's gone, Vinnie." Larry dropped down and began digging in the snow.

Vinnie looked around the area. "Somebody

found him. Look." He pointed to large boot tracks leading away from them. The tread didn't fit either of their snow boots. "Somebody carried him off."

"They didn't take him back to the lodge, or we would have seen them," said Larry.

"A sleigh," said Vinnie. "Here are the tracks leading that way." He pointed into the woods.

"A sleigh? You mean like Santa Claus?" Larry looked heavenward.

"Yeah, doofus. Santa came down and picked him up. And he'll get the diamond if we don't find them first. Come on."

They followed the tracks of a one horse sleigh as it disappeared into the forest. It wasn't long before they came across a tiny cabin. A thin wisp of smoke was coming out of the chimney. Vinnie and Larry slowly approached the small house and peered in the grimy front window.

A man in a red parka huddled near a small fire burning in the fireplace. His back was to the window. There wasn't anyone else in the cabin.

"He must have gotten rid of the body and stole his jacket," whispered Vinnie.

"Did he take the ring?" asked Larry.

"I can't tell. Come on," he said, marching toward the door. "It's two against one."

Vinnie pushed open the door. The man by the fireplace jumped to his feet and turned around.

"It's you," said Larry, recognizing the man from the snowdrift.

"Thank God, you found me," said the man. "I thought I'd be out here till the spring thaw. But I didn't hear your car."

"We walked," said Larry.

"You walked? How far away from the lodge are we?"

"Not far," said Vinnie, looking around the room. A wooden table and two chairs sat under the window. A well-worn couch rested in front of the fireplace. Some cabinets, open and bare, were against another wall. He noticed an old set of fireplace tools on the wide hearth.

"What happened?" Larry asked.

"I had a seizure on the upper road. I passed out and must have rolled down the hill. I came to under a big tree and heard bells. One of the sleigh horses from the lodge must have gotten loose and was breathing in my face. I hoped the horse would get me back to the hotel, but we ended up here. I unhitched him and put him in the shed out back, came in the cabin, and built the fire."

"Why don't you warm up a little more before we head back," said Vinnie, inching his way toward the hearth.

"Great idea. I like cold weather, but this was a little much, even for me." He sat on the couch and gazed into the fire.

Larry plopped down next to the man. The firelight enhanced the deep wrinkles on the guy's forehead and the crinkles around his eyes. "How do you feel?" he asked, leaning closer to get a better view of the older man.

"I feel fine now." He turned and looked at Larry. "I can't believe you two walked out in the snow to find me. Not many strangers would put themselves out like that."

"We found your wallet in the snow," blurted Larry. "Didn't we, Vinnie?"

Vinnie had his hand nearly around the fireplace poker. He jerked up straight. "Yeah. Here it is." He dug into his jacket pocket. "I had to go through everything to see who owned it. You didn't have any credit cards."

"Never use them," said the man, leaning forward, taking the wallet. He stuffed it in his pants pocket without going through the cash. "Thanks so much. You two really are extraordinary. It does my heart good to see two guys who are down on their luck being so honest."

Vinnie tried covering up the hole in his ill-fitting parka while Larry tugged at the faulty zipper of his own jacket.

"You could have done a lot with that money. I owe you."

"We don't want anything," said Larry. "We're just glad you're okay."

"We should go now," said Vinnie.

The man stood. He was a bit rocky on his feet. Larry slid an arm around his back and helped steady him.

"Thank you, son. What time is it?" He looked at

In the Nick of Time

his watch. It was an expensive gold one. Vinnie and Larry caught a glimpse of the big diamond ring on his finger, too. It was so heavy, it rolled to one side. "Getting on to dinnertime. I hope they have something hearty tonight at the lodge. I could eat a bear." He gave a deep laugh that rumbled through the cabin.

They stepped outside. A cold wind whipped through the trees and bit their faces. Dark clouds were rolling in like a tidal wave.

"Go hitch up the sleigh, Larry," said Vinnie.

"Why don't you come with me, Vinnie?" Larry's eyes jumped between his partner and the older man with the white beard who was leaning against the porch railing.

"You do it. We'll stay here."

Larry's eyes dropped to Vinnie's empty hands.

"Okay. Don't... go anywhere."

Larry hitched up and then led the horse drawn sleigh to the front of the small log cabin.

"Let me put out the fire," said Vinnie. "I'll be back in a minute." He went into the cabin and partially shut the door.

As Larry was going to help the man into the sled, he asked, "What's your name?"

"Nicholas. You can call me Nick."

"Nick? Like St. Nick? And look, it's Christmas Eve. Gee." Larry lowered his head and fiddled with the reins for a second. "I'm glad you're not... I'm glad you are all right. How many kids you got?"

Nick wasn't listening. He had turned his head

and was looking at the door behind him. "Give me a second."

He pushed inside the cabin.

"Vinnie? That's your name, isn't it?" he said to Vinnie's back. The heavyset guy with the greasy black hair turned around. "I want to thank you for all you've done." He reached into his pocket and pulled out the wallet. "Here. Take this." He handed Vinnie all the bills. "It's not much, but... I don't know. Maybe it's the season, but thanks. Split it with your buddy." He stared at the man standing by the fireplace. Vinnie looked away and shuffled his feet. "Lesser men would have kept the money. I've learned something from you."

He folded Vinnie's hand over the bills, turned, and walked out on the porch. He was in the sleigh beside Larry when Vinnie stepped outside.

Vinnie climbed aboard, took the reins, and they went back to the lodge.

Everyone else must have been out in the snow looking for the lost man, because there were no people clustered around the front door.

"Let me off at the side door, fellas," said Nick. "I want to go to my room first." He got out and went in the service entrance while Vinnie and Larry took the sleigh around to the rear and left it with a young stable boy near the barn.

Then the pair went inside the lodge.

They were wrong about everyone being out searching for the missing man. The huge open room with the biggest fireplace was full of people, all talking at once, happy and excited. Mrs. Whitman walked amongst the crowd, shaking their hands, tears in her eyes, but she was overjoyed.

She finally got over to where the pair was standing. "Thank you. Thank you. He's fine. I appreciate all your help. Everyone has been so nice."

"I'm glad Nick is okay," said Larry.

"Nick? My husband's name is John. You do know the ranger found him at the wayfarer's chapel down the road. He had been mugged, robbed."

"Robbed?" questioned Vinnie.

"Yes. The thief stole his parka and scarf and made off with his money and jewelry. But John's safe."

The man in the blue ski sweater stepped up to Mrs. Whitman. "It was some slick dude with a beard. He's been working the ski lodges up here. It's a gold mine for thieves."

The next morning a small wrapped parcel was found under the large evergreen tree in the lobby of the lodge. It was addressed to John Whitman. It contained a handful of credit cards, a gold watch, and a diamond ring. A note was attached.

It said: *Merry Christmas—Nick*

Copyright © 2008 Gayle Bartos-Pool

Team Player

Marian Allen

It was Christmas at Cranston's, a department store too upscale to identify itself as one. It had become, like other superstars, a one-name entity.

Helen Dasher, petite and slender with delicate wrists and ankles, rose from her office chair. She wore fawn-colored slacks and jacket, and a white blouse. Her feet, in black high heels, were nearly invisible, only the toes of her shiny pumps showing, like glossy hooves. As she crossed the room to her boss and the man he was showing around, her heels went *click, click, click*.

"Toys," Mr. Cranston said to the man standing next to him. "Toys are what the store is all about during the Christmas season, and Helen Dasher is Toys. Helen, this is Ralph Basco, our new Sales Manager."

Basco had dark, coarse hair and yellow eyes. He sized Helen up with an appreciative leer that froze her in her tracks.

Mr. Cranston clapped Basco on the shoulder. "Ralph is tops in his field. We were lucky to steal him from Markson's. We'll increase our profits—how much did you project?"

"Fifteen percent per quarter." Basco shook a finger at Mr. Cranston in playful warning. "But only if you follow my advice."

Cranston pulled out his pocket handkerchief and wiped his hands with it. "Er... Helen, Ralph here thinks we should change our buying strategy for the toys next year. Too late for this year, of course—"

"Called me in too late," Basco agreed.

Helen was warily conscious of Basco as she objected. "Change our buying strategy? In what way? Our toy sales have always—"

"Been good, but Ralph says we can do better. Not your fault, Helen, no reflection on you. You're a buyer, and Ralph's a seller. This is what we pay him to do. Right, Ralph?"

"Right, Mr. C. And I believe in doing what I'm paid to do."

* * *

Neither Helen nor her friends did their Christmas shopping at Cranston's. Not all children would wake up, like the children of Cranston's privileged customers, to new skis and tickets to Switzerland. Helen and her friends spent their Christmas savings at sales and discount stores. They saw to it that the least fortunate children on their list— children they had never met—woke up to something, even if it were only a candy cane and a plastic truck. Too bad Santa's workshop full of busy little elves was only a fiction.

Helen stepped into the elevator and punched the button for the toy department.

When the doors opened, Ray Donner, Assistant Sales Manager and Helen's dearest friend, stood waiting for her. He was trim and athletic, with soulful brown eyes. He and Helen had grown up together, working side-by-side since the day they'd entered harness.

"Met my new boss? Basco?" he asked.

Helen snorted. "I met him. As if it weren't bad enough they passed you over to hire him, he's trying to talk Mr. Cranston into decisions I know are wrong...."

Ray smiled. "You know I don't care about the promotion, don't you? I've never been a leader."

"Yes, I know. Still, it doesn't do the team any good to have an outsider brought in ahead of them. Oh, we know it works out sometimes, but only when the whole team sees the need, and this is not one of those times. The man is a predator, besides." Helen remembered Basco's hungry once-over and shivered in revulsion.

Donner shook his head. "If Mr. Cranston wants to pay for bad advice, that's his decision. It's his company. As for his wolfishness...." He grinned. "He wouldn't be the first wolf who learned that inoffensive doesn't mean defenseless."

* * *

Ralph Basco rubbed his bruised cheek. "Just before Christmas would be a bad time to lose your job. You have a fist like a rock!"

"And this company has a zero-tolerance policy toward sexual harassment." Helen straightened her blouse.

"Don't kid yourself, honey. Buyers are thick on the ground." He patted his chest and said, "Ralph Basco is going to pull this company out of a three-year sales slump. Go on—report me. The worst I'll get is a slap on the wrist."

"There hasn't been a sales slump in Toys. My department has been carrying this company through these hard times—"

"That's what *you* say. That isn't what *I* say. And I came very highly priced. I had to be bought away from a rival company. That means what I say must be right."

Grinning, Ralph ran a finger down Helen's jawline. She cocked her fist for another lesson in respecting personal space, but Ralph's cell phone rang.

"Later," he told her, and turned his back. Into the phone, he said, "Just a minute," and waited to hear her leave.

She walked out, her heels silent on the carpet. She closed the door until it latched, then eased it open and listened, ears almost visibly pricked forward.

"Going great," Ralph said. "According to plan, and ahead of schedule. I think I can talk him into dumping most of his top sellers in a pre-Christmas sale, then using the money to pick up some 'sleepers' that—between the two of us—he couldn't give away." Ralph laughed. "Thank you, Mr. Markson. I believe in doing what I'm paid to do."

Helen knew the official channels weren't going to work when Mr. Cranston called her into his office, turned her report on Basco's double-dealing face-down, and refused to meet her eyes.

"Helen…." He cleared his throat. "You've been with the company a long time. You're a valuable member of our team. I think you know that."

"But...," she prompted.

"But Ralph is valuable, too. We expect great things out of him. I'm deeply disappointed in this." He tapped the back of her private memo.

"Disappointed in me?"

"I know you have grievances against Basco, but to make an accusation like this...."

"What about it?" Helen understood, when Mr. Cranston said nothing . "You don't believe it, do you—that he's working for Markson? You think I invented it, to get back at him for taking Ray Donner's job and undercutting mine."

"And then there's this harassment complaint. Don't you think you're over-reacting? You're an attractive person; naturally other people are going to notice and pay you the occasional compliment. Is that so terrible?"

"So if a wolf takes a big bite out of your butt, is that a compliment to how good you taste? Are you flattered?"

"The shareholders...." Beads of sweat popped out on Cranston's bald head and ran down into his collar.

She picked up her report and her complaint, tore the papers in half, in half again, and dropped the pieces in Cranston's waste basket.

* * *

Ray Donner joined her for lunch in the break room. He held up half his vegetarian sub. "Share?"

She took it, and scraped half of her salad onto his plate.

"It didn't go well, I take it," Donner said softly.

"I'll be lucky if I don't start the new year on the unemployment line."

"I wish I could back you up, but he's been very cautious around me. The proof will be next quarter's report. That'll show the damage, but you can bet he won't take any of the blame. It'll be my fault, and yours, and Mr. Cranston's, and Ralph Basco will end up looking like a star athlete with a bad team behind him."

"He isn't becoming 'enlightened,' either," Helen said. "He gets worse." She put down her fork. "You won't believe this: He's made a date with himself to come to my house tonight. I told him I wouldn't be there, and he wanted to know when I'd be back. I lied and said I'd be out all night, and he just grinned and said he'd drive by, and if my car wasn't there he'd see me tomorrow night. He implied I'd better be there tonight, though."

"Or what?"

"Or, I suppose, I will start the new year unemployed, with a lousy reference or even word on the corporate grapevine that I'm poison to a company. I can start over again in some other town or some other career, but at what salary? How long will it take me to work my way back up to current earnings?" She lowered her head. "I don't care for me—it's the kids." The kids were what she worked for all year, what her closest friends worked for all year: the kids who wouldn't have a Christmas without them.

"Well, then." Ray's tone gave the two words the finality of a judgement from the bench.

Helen looked up. "Are you saying what I think you're saying?"

"I'll make a few calls. It won't be the first time we've had to rally 'round, and it won't be the last. But it's your decision. You say."

Helen took a bite of salad and chewed slowly, thoughtfully.

Then she nodded.

* * *

"Thought you were going out tonight, honey." Ralph stood grinning on the porch. "Aren't you going to invite me in? Or you want to go out somewhere first?" He waved a hand toward the black Corvette he'd parked behind her own modest Datsun.

Helen stepped aside so he could enter.

"Cute place," Basco said, as she closed the door. He sat on the couch, stretching an arm along the back. She sat in a chair across the room. Ralph laughed. "Okay, straight talk: Between the two of us, you're good at your job. But good at your job isn't enough today. You have to be smart. You have to play the game. Get me?"

"Is that how they do things at Markson's?"

Ralph's smile turned furtive. "I don't work for Markson's any more."

"I know better."

"Did you tell Mr. Cranston? Did it help?

Welcome to the wicked world, little girl. The good guys don't always win. Santa Claus isn't real, either, I hate to be the one to tell you."

Helen's phone rang.

She reached for the handset, but Ralph growled, "Let the machine get it," and she sat back.

After the beep, strident tones bleated, "Sweetie, this is Vixie from across the street. I know you're there, I can see your car. I just thought you might like to know they're towing that black Corvette outta your driveway."

"WHAT?!" Ralph was out before Vixie had hung up. He left the door standing open.

"You'd think he was born in a barn." Helen looked out. The street light shone on a red tow truck with **COMET SALVAGE AND TOWING** painted on the door panel, the black Corvette dangling from its winch. Ralph ran alongside, shouting into the driver's window, until the truck pulled away, tugging Ralph's car behind it.

Ralph thundered up the steps. "Says he's towing for the city. Mix-up with the tags. I gotta get to the impound yard. Drive me, honey?"

"I've called you a cab."

"I'll see you tomorrow, maybe come back tonight, if I can get this mess straightened out." he reached for her, but Helen stepped away. Ralph grinned. "Play it that way, then."

A horn blared in the street.

"That was quick."

The cab was as red as the tow truck. A sign on

top said **KRINGLE AND KRINGLE, GIVE US A JINGLE**—*CALL 555-NICE*. A little old driver hopped out and scurried around to open the passenger door.

"Ready for the holidays?" he asked Ralph.

"Yeah, yeah. Let's just step on it, okay?"

"Okay with me." The driver closed Ralph into the cab.

The cabbie scampered around to his door, tucking his long white beard into the front of his scarlet windbreaker.

Ray Donner and Vixie came out of the house across the street and, with Helen Dasher, watched Ralph get into the taxi. The cabbie waved to them. They waved back.

(Witnesses would testify to seeing Ralph in another part of the city later that night—a German businessman named Hans Blitzen; Starr Dancer, an "exotic artiste" at the Teddy Bear Club; Qupe and Pranzr Dehr, tourists; and "Red" Rudolph, a former linebacker for Minnesota. Ralph's disappearance would never be solved, though—not until polar bears learned to talk.)

"And I heard him exclaim, as he drove out of sight," Donner said, "'Don't let the bastards wear you down!'"

Dasher laughed. It was great to be part of a team.

Copyright © 2008 Marian Allen

Contributor Profiles

Here are short biographical sketches of each anthology contributor. Support these worthy and generous souls by dropping by their websites if they have them and perhaps purchasing their other books!

Marian Allen - Marian Allen writes science fiction, fantasy, mystery, humor, horror, mainstream, and anything else she can wrestle into fixed form. She has had stories in on-line and print publications, on coffee cans and the wall of an Indian restaurant in Louisville, Kentucky. She writes a daily food history column for Worldwide Recipes.com and blogs on **FatalFoodies.blogspot.com**. Allen is a member of the Green River Writers and the Southern Indiana Writers Group.

Janice Alonso - Janice Alonso writes mystery, children's, and literary short stories as well as inspirational articles. Her work is included in *Blessings for Mothers*, *Chicken Soup for the Christian Soul 2*, and *Chicken Soup for the Beach Lover's Soul*. Her work has also appeared in *Crime & Suspense, Grit, Anthology, Palo Alto Review, The Storyteller, Primary Treasure, The Lutheran Digest, Spirituality for Today, Foliate Oak Magazine*, and others. Visit her at **www.janicealonso.com**.

Allan E. Ansorge - Raised in a farming community in rural Wisconsin, Allan did not see a library until he was forced on to a bus to attend high school. There he was kidnapped forever by Holmes and Christie. After a successful career, and business ownership he has returned to his vocation of choice. Spreading imagination and humor on pages to the enjoyment of those who wait patiently to see, What Happens Next?

Gayle Bartos-Pool - A former private detective and a reporter for a small weekly newspaper, Gayle has one published book, *Media Justice*, and several short stories in anthologies, *LAndmarked for Murder* and *Little Sisters Volume 1*. She is currently the Speakers Bureau Director for Sisters in Crime/Los Angeles, and a member of Mystery Writers of America. Visit her at **www.gbpool.com**

Tony Burton - Tony has worn a lot of hats in his life, including a sailor's "dixie cup." He is a Navy veteran of twelve-plus years, an ex-teacher, ex-journalist and ex-computer consultant. Tony has two published novels, and his short stories and articles have appeared in anthologies, magazines and newspapers. Presently he devotes his workdays to writing, teaching creative writing and running his publishing business, and his "free time" (hah!) to building a new home in North Georgia with his lovely wife. Visit him at **www.tonyburton.biz**.

Austin S. Camacho - Austin is a 53-year-old communications specialist for the Department of Defense with five novels in print. He lives in northern Virginia with his wife, Denise, and when he is not writing enjoys running along the shores of the Potomac, watching action films, and shooting — at paper targets, not live ones. He is a voracious reader of just about any kind of nonfiction, plus mysteries, adventures and thrillers. Visit him at **www.ascamacho.com**

S. M. Harding - S. M. Harding has had short mystery fiction published in *Detective Mystery Stories*, *Great Mystery and Suspense Magazine*, *Crime and Suspense* ezine, and *Mysterical-E*, as well as the anthologies *Racing Can Be Murder* and *Medium of Murder*. She lives in Indianapolis and has finished a novel entitled *The Shadow of Truth*.

Peg Herring - Peg is a former educator and the author of the historical novel *Macbeth's Niece* as well as plays, short stories, and articles. Her upcoming novel with Five Star, *Her Highness' First Murder*, is a mystery centered on young Elizabeth Tudor. In addition to writing Peg loves public speaking, travel, and music. She sings solos in transit but never in public. Visit her website at **www.pegherring.com**

Gary R. Hoffman - After quitting the teaching rat race for 22 years, Gary now lives in a motor home, travels the North American Continent, and says "Home is where you park it!" He has published over 200 short stories and has won or placed in many contests for short stories. Visit him at **www.garyrhoffman.com**

M. E. Kemp - M. E. write historical mysteries with two nosy puritans as detectives. Her latest book, Death of a Bawdy Belle, is set in Salem during the witch trials. She researched Dutch customs for her book, Death of a Dutch Uncle. Her short stories appear in many anthologies. Born in Oxford, MA, a town her ancestors settled in 1713, Kemp now lives in Sarasota Springs, NY. She is pleased to support the Toys for Tots. Visit her at **www.mekemp.com**

Terrie Farley Moran - A life-long New Yorker, Terrie dabbles in genealogy and is learning to play the Irish Tin Whistle, which she finds far more troublesome than babysitting for her ever-increasing number of grandchildren. Her short story "Strike Zone" can be found in the SinC anthology, *Murder New York Style*. Terrie invites one and all to drop by **www.womenofmystery.net** to enjoy the grand blogging banter of six talented New York mystery writers.

Radine Trees Nehring - Radine spent ten years as a broadcast journalist and magazine feature writer before her first book, *DEAR EARTH: A Love Letter from Spring Hollow*, appeared in 1995, winning the Arkansas Governor's Award for best writing about the state. Her mystery series began in 2002 with Macavity nominee, *A Valley to Die For*. The series has earned many other awards, including Arkansas Book of the Year. The fifth series novel, *A River to Die For*, was released in April, 2008. Visit her at **www.radinesbooks.com**

Helen Schwartz - Helen explores locales around Washington, D.C., for her murder mysteries—cheering dragon boat races on the Potomac, researching at the Folger Shakespeare Library, and haunting the centuries-old Congressional Cemetery for her book *The Wrong Vampire*. A Professor Emerita at Indiana University in Indianapolis, she teaches online courses on outcome-based assessment, lectures on Shakespeare and the Internet, and serves as vice president of the Chesapeake Chapter of Sisters in Crime. She spins a mean dreydl.

Printed in the United States
204777BV00001B/148-543/P